"About last night. I hope you aren't upset."

"I'm not going to run screaming into the woods just because you kissed me," Jane said tartly.

"Good," he told her, "because if you did, I'd have to chase you down and use all my powers of persuasion to bring you back."

"Is that a threat or a promise?"

"A promise. And I have a lot of powers of persuasion." So did she, Luke conceded silently. "Being around a baby brings a glow to your face. Did you know that?" Without thinking, he reached toward her…

And received a fidgeting Tina in response. "Holding an infant makes a man irresistible," she replied. "To any female from nine to ninety."

Dear Reader,

Jane McKay, the obstetrician who longs for a baby of her own, deserved her own book after playing a role in three earlier stories set in the Harmony Circle neighborhood in Brea, California. Since Jane is down-to-earth and dresses simply, she's never seen herself as a love match for charismatic lady-killer Luke Van Dam, the fellow OB she had a crush on when they studied together in medical school.

Now, divorced and irresistible as ever, he's become not only her new medical partner but her next-door neighbor. She can't refuse to help when he unexpectedly gets custody of two little girls, but how utterly unfair that not only did he steal her heart, he also acquires children without even trying.

I'm rooting for Jane, and I hope you will, too. As for Luke, well, he stole my heart, as well. Hope you'll enjoy this tale of a sexy man in a white coat!

Best,

Jacqueline Diamond

Doctor Daddy

JACQUELINE DIAMOND

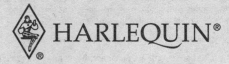

TORONTO • NEW YORK • LONDON
AMSTERDAM • PARIS • SYDNEY • HAMBURG
STOCKHOLM • ATHENS • TOKYO • MILAN • MADRID
PRAGUE • WARSAW • BUDAPEST • AUCKLAND

Recycling programs for this product may not exist in your area.

ISBN-13: 978-0-373-75277-5

DOCTOR DADDY

This edition published by arrangement with Harlequin Books S.A.

® and TM are trademarks of the publisher. Trademarks indicated with ® are registered in the United States Patent and Trademark Office, the Canadian Trade Marks Office and in other countries.

www.eHarlequin.com

Printed in U.S.A.

ABOUT THE AUTHOR

Jacqueline Diamond, the author of more than eighty novels, has survived raising two sons in an Orange County, California, community similar to Harmony Circle. Having celebrated their thirtieth anniversary, she and her husband bear testimony to the enduring power of love. Jackie welcomes reader correspondence at jdiamondfriends@yahoo.com, and provides updated information on her activities at www.jacquelinediamond.com.

Books by Jacqueline Diamond

HARLEQUIN AMERICAN ROMANCE

*Downhome Doctors
†Harmony Circle

For my mother, artist Sylvia Hyman,
a role model for how to live fully
through her eighties and into her nineties.

Chapter One

Only a few hours old, the infant scrunched her eyes and yawned, oblivious to the humming noises of the nursery and the rows of bassinets around her. With the tiniest of wriggling motions, she nestled into Dr. Jane McKay's arms.

Jane's heart squeezed. She'd delivered three babies this morning, including the little angel she was cradling. If only one of them were hers.

She did have time to bear a baby of her own. Just not a *lot* of time, with her thirty-fifth birthday little more than a month away.

After that, as Jane often informed patients, her fertility would decline sharply with every passing year, and the risk of pregnancy complications would increase. Of course, modern medicine offered almost miraculous advances and some high-tech alternatives to the conventional route of man, marriage and motherhood.

She still hoped, in her more optimistic moods, that she would find the right guy. Sure, she met plenty of men, but no one she felt she could share her life and future with. So as the months and years ticked by, she'd been giving more and more thought to having a baby on her own.

Scary, exciting thought.

Jane returned her attention to the small, alert face with its rosebud mouth. How utterly innocent this baby girl looked, how warm and responsive and…

Flirtatious?

While she knew the infant's unfocused eyes couldn't see into the hallway beyond the observation window, Jane glanced curiously to where she was gazing. On the far side of the glass, framed by the red hearts the North Orange County Medical Center staff had posted for Valentine's Day, she spotted a pair of wide shoulders and a head of perfectly styled golden-brown hair.

She didn't immediately recognize the man. But her body flushed instinctively, and out of the past popped a name.

Oh, who was she kidding? No woman ever forgot Luke Van Dam. Not even Jane, and heaven knew, she'd tried.

He stood, half turned away from her, talking to someone. For a weak moment, Jane enjoyed looking at the broad back of the sexiest man she'd ever met, while her memory filled in the details. A cleft that flashed in his left cheek at rare moments. Gray eyes that on closer inspection revealed rays of violet. A hard mouth that could soften into a heart-stopping smile.

She hadn't seen him since they'd been classmates and members of the same study group at UCLA's medical school. The last she'd heard, he'd been practicing in Los Angeles, an hour's drive from her home here in the town of Brea. Only an hour, but a different world.

What was he doing here?

When he shifted position, she glimpsed a slim brunette nurse absorbed in conversation with him. Judging by her rapt expression, Jane could see that the passage of time hadn't diminished the spell Luke cast.

Against Jane's shoulder, the baby uttered a contented sigh. Oh, honestly. The little one's happiness *couldn't* have anything to do with the great Dr. Van Dam, even if his classmates had teased him about being the ultimate babe magnet.

Irked by her reaction to the man, Jane tucked the baby back into her bassinet and checked on the other infants she'd delivered. Although their welfare was no longer her responsibility, she enjoyed this chance to observe the tiny people whose hearts she'd been listening to and whose minute forms she'd been studying via ultrasound for so many months. Plus, an extra pair of trained eyes never hurt. Only last week she'd spotted a developing case of jaundice so new even the nurse hadn't yet noticed. Treatment with phototherapy had cleared it up.

Nurturing women and their babies had been Jane's dream from an early age. She wanted to be there for them, using her talent and training to improve their lives and, sometimes, even save them. And she was living that dream.

In the anteroom, the clock read 3:15 p.m. Jane shed her protective clothing, washed her hands and went out. She'd had to postpone a couple of appointments due to today's births, but she'd still be able to keep her four o'clock and four-thirty. Jane hated inconveniencing patients.

No sign of Luke in the hall. Perhaps he'd dropped by to see his younger cousin, Sean Sawyer, who was Jane's medical partner. She'd almost forgotten the men were related. Both turned female heads wherever they went but, despite Sean's good looks, he'd never quickened Jane's pulse.

Who could account for taste? Jane wished hers didn't fall into line with that of so many others. Luke had always held an almost mesmeric attraction for nurses, fellow medical students and women in general. And Jane.

For their first three years as study partners, she'd been his friend, and in some ways, as they bolstered each other through medical school, she'd come to know him better than anyone.

Then, one night when they took a break from hours of studying, she'd foolishly acted on her feelings. Big mistake. Not that Luke had behaved like a jerk, exactly. He'd made it clear he'd had a good time and wouldn't mind a rematch.

A rematch! Like an idiot, she'd been hoping he'd feel a lot more. Maybe even as much as she did. Almost as upset with herself as with him, Jane had kept her distance.

That was almost ten years ago. She only wished seeing him again hadn't thrown her into a state of confusion.

She left the hospital via a side door and set out on foot for her office a block away. Along the path, calla lilies and pansies bloomed in the late-afternoon sunshine. Jane still relished Southern California's splendid February weather even though it was almost a dozen years since she'd moved here from her hometown of Cincinnati, Ohio.

A dental clinic and an optometry office flanked her medical suite, which she entered through a private door. In the changing room, she donned a fresh white coat and ran a brush through the shoulder-length light brown hair that she'd been growing out for the past eight months.

After checking with her nurse, Rosemary Tran, Jane approved several refill prescriptions. Rosemary also reported a couple of nonemergency calls from patients. Pregnant women craved reassurance, and, besides, an apparently minor symptom could indicate more serious problems best nipped in the bud.

Jane returned both calls before her four-o'clock patient arrived, an older woman recovering from a hysterectomy. Jane spent extra time reviewing such issues as her sex drive, hot flashes and bone density. All seemed in order.

The four-thirty appointment canceled, so the extended discussion didn't inconvenience anyone. En route to her private office to dictate her notes, Jane spotted receptionist Edda Jonas, whose round, freckled face glowed even pinker than usual.

"Have you seen… Oh, I wish they'd explain what… Well, I guess they're waiting for you," Edda babbled.

"Excuse me?" Jane tried in vain to sort out this burst of words.

"They're in Dr. Sawyer's office. I didn't think anybody could be better-looking, but…well, he's—he's just…" A deep breath barely saved Edda from a meltdown.

No question who had inspired that burst of feminine enthusiasm. "I assume you're referring to Dr. Van Dam."

Edda nodded mutely.

Clearly the man had taken her breath away. "I'd better go say hello."

"Is he… He's not wearing a ring, but I wondered…"

"I have no idea if he's married." She'd purposely avoided asking Sean anything about him.

As the receptionist went back to her desk, Jane

wondered if this visit had anything to do with the recent death of Sean's great-aunt. Last week, he'd attended her funeral in Santa Barbara, north of L.A. Perhaps the cousins had rekindled their friendship after the service, but if so, why were they meeting up on a workday?

She ducked into the restroom to freshen her lipstick. Silly to worry about such a thing, but she needed a moment to prepare for seeing Luke.

She'd worked hard to recover from her misplaced attraction years ago, but her response at the hospital made it clear that she hadn't entirely succeeded. Really, Jane told herself sternly, they'd both moved past that incident. There was no reason for any discomfort between them—or any primping on her part, either.

Drawing herself to her full five-foot-seven-inch height—make that five-nine in pumps—she proceeded down the hall. As she raised her hand to knock on Sean's door, deep laughter drifted out. A tingle ran from the soles of her feet up to her earlobes.

Get over it, McKay.

She rapped. A moment later, the door swung open to reveal Sean's welcoming smile. "Good! You're here." He ushered her inside. "You remember my cousin Luke?"

Instantly, his heady masculine scent made her feel like a first-year med student, trying not to gawk at the gorgeous man who'd somehow joined her study group. His mere presence reshaped Sean's office, recasting the angles and sharpening the colors. A hint of cragginess had replaced the smoothness of youth in his strong-boned face, yet she caught a startling flash of vulnerability in that violet gaze.

He was almost irresistible, the key word being *almost*.

Jane extended her hand, which he enfolded in his. "Of course I remember him," she said briskly. "In fact, I saw you at the hospital, Luke. Sorry I didn't get a chance to say hello."

"It's a terrific facility." He released her with a trace of reluctance. Chalk that up to his instinctive bedside manner. "The new birthing center is impressive."

"You sound as if you were evaluating it. Surely you're not planning to practice here," Jane commented more tartly than she'd intended. When he blinked, she realized her words might sound unfriendly. "I mean, our little med center can't measure up to the facilities in L.A." He'd always been ambitious, and the last she'd heard, he'd been affiliated with a major teaching hospital.

The men exchanged looks. *Something* was definitely afoot.

"Actually, Luke's doing me—doing us both—a favor," Sean blurted. "Jane, I just found out that I've inherited money from Aunt Mattie. Enough to discharge my student loans. I've been talking your ear off about working in an impoverished area. Well, I can finally afford to do it."

Jane struggled to absorb this turn of events. She'd long been aware of, and admired, Sean's ambition to go overseas to help poor women. But they'd both assumed it would be years before he paid off those bills.

So his aunt Mattie had left him a legacy. That was wonderful, both because he could now reach for his dream and because Jane understood the relief of climbing out from under crushing debt. She would always be grateful to her own mother for making sure that, after her death following a long illness, the insurance was enough to pay off Jane's loans and provide a down payment on a house. Nothing could replace her mother, but Jane didn't miss those sleepless nights worrying about her financial burden.

Then the rest of her partner's statement sank in. *Luke's doing me—doing us both—a favor.* He planned to work here, with her?

Good heavens. Not that she couldn't deal with the situation. Jane had long ago left her youthful insecurities behind. But why on earth would Luke, who hungered for major research projects and challenging surgeries, want to move to a small town?

The men stood watching her, obviously awaiting her reaction. "Congratulations," she told Sean. "When do you think you'll go?"

"At the beginning of March."

That was two weeks away. "How'd you find a position so fast?"

"I already planned to work at a mission in Central America for a few weeks this summer, remember?"

"Well, sure." He'd mentioned traveling with an international group that brought its own medical equipment and supplies.

"After I learned of Aunt Mattie's bequest, I called the mission to see if they could use a doctor on a long-term basis." Excitement tinged Sean's voice. "It turns out they just got a grant to open a full-service clinic and they need a director, preferably an ob-gyn. Luke's offered to fill in here for a year. Isn't that fantastic?"

"It sure is." Finding a replacement of Luke's caliber *was* a stroke of good fortune. "But how can you relocate on such short notice? And why would you want to?"

"That's my Jane," Luke said fondly. "Blunt as ever. Glad to see you haven't changed."

His Jane? She hadn't imagined he ever thought of her that way. Or that he thought of her at all.

You're making too much of this, McKay.

"That isn't an answer," she replied calmly. "What's going on?"

"I've been looking to move to North Orange County for personal reasons." Luke offered no further explanation.

Personal… Well, he had a right to his privacy. Jane, too, preferred to keep this relationship strictly professional. "You're starting in two weeks?"

"That's the plan," he said. "If it's okay with you."

"No problem. Glad to have you on board." No problem except that, against her will, her body vibrated with his nearness. Plus the fact that she'd felt uneasy around him ever since that night almost ten years ago, even though he hadn't seemed to notice. "Transitions can be hard on patients. Who's going to notify them? Pam?" Pam Ortiz was Sean's nurse.

"I'll phone them myself," Sean promised. "We'll make this as smooth as possible."

"I'm sorry you're leaving, even though it's for such a good cause." With complete sincerity, Jane added, "I'll miss you."

Although they'd never socialized, they'd shared a vision for their practice and their community. When brush fires destroyed homes in nearby Yorba Linda and turned the Brea Community Center into a temporary shelter, the two of them had spent most of the weekend counseling evacuees and offering medical services. Fortunately, there'd been no fire-related injuries, but a couple of pregnant women had thanked them for the attention.

When Sean gave her a hug, he felt solid and comforting. "It's been great working together."

"You're not kidding." Realizing she hadn't exactly welcomed Luke, Jane turned to him. "I'm sure we'll make a fine team."

"I know I can count on you," he told her. To Sean, he explained, "In med school, when the rest of us were freaking out about exams, she always kept us focused." Late-afternoon sunlight softened the chiseled planes of his face and the slight crookedness of his nose. An old football injury, she recalled.

"Jane's not only one of the best doctors around, she's also a font of wisdom on all sorts of subjects," Sean remarked. "Did you realize she worked her way through college as a nanny?"

"Before medical school," Jane added in response to Luke's puzzled expression. As a med student, she'd found hospital-related jobs.

She'd never mentioned being a nanny because there'd been a subtle jockeying for status among the future doctors. Many had come from wealthy or professional families, and being the daughter of a truck driver had already put Jane at a disadvantage.

Luke raised an eyebrow. "Sounds like a good way to learn about mothers and their needs."

"It was."

Sean went on praising his partner. "And she knows practically everything about Brea. She's a great resource."

"As a matter of fact—" Luke's velvet gaze fixed on

Jane "—I need to find a rental, and Sean's apartment is a bit small. Any suggestions?"

"You should talk to Oliver Armstrong at Archway Real Estate." Oliver and his wife, Brooke, lived next door to Jane and had become close friends. "The last I heard, he was looking to rent a condo he owns about a mile from here."

The unit lay within walking distance of shops, cinemas and a comedy club. It ought to be perfect for a bachelor who entertained hot-and-cold-running women. Make that hot, exclusively.

Unless Luke was married. To her annoyance, she had to fight not to glance at his left hand. But then, Edda had already mentioned he didn't wear a ring.

"Archway Real Estate," he repeated. "I'll get in touch."

They shook hands and Jane went to her office. Since it was after five, she dictated her notes quickly and departed.

As she drove the short distance to her Harmony Circle neighborhood, her thoughts sparked against each other. Unbelievable. Luke the Duke, as the female med students used to call him, was going to be her partner.

She intended to take the situation in stride. But right now, she wasn't sure whether that meant walking sedately, loping for an exit or running for her life.

Chapter Two

"You should confide in her," Sean told Luke when they were alone. "I can't imagine anyone more trustworthy than Jane."

"I will, eventually. It's not as if Zoey's a secret." Luke tried not to be too obvious as he scanned the small office that, in a couple of weeks, would be his. There was barely room for a desk, a couple of chairs and a small couch. He'd have to leave half his medical books at home, he calculated, but then, it was easier to consult references via computer, anyway. Harder to leave behind were some clinical trials he'd had to withdraw from, although fortunately he'd found another doctor to continue his work uninterrupted. "I just want to be discreet while I sort things out."

"I got it." Sean flashed him a grin. "Hey, I bet you're a great dad."

"I'm trying to be." Luke didn't care to elaborate. His cousin meant well, but although only two years younger, the guy still radiated innocent eagerness. For Luke, life had become much more complicated.

Once upon a time, he too had brimmed with optimism. Unlike Sean, though, he'd been self-absorbed and cocky. Well, life had taught him a few lessons.

During his residency, Luke had dated Pauline Rogers, a vivacious singer. He'd enjoyed her energy and zest, and basked in the reflected limelight during her performances at L.A. clubs.

Then she got pregnant. Although neither of them felt ready for marriage, they'd said their vows and done their best to make things work. After the birth of their little girl, Luke—exhausted from long hours at the hospital—never realized how much his wife chafed at taking a break from her career. He'd come home with only enough energy to cuddle their daughter briefly before collapsing into bed.

They'd divorced three years ago. Luke had fought for custody, but the judge had sided with the mother, taking into account Luke's long hours at work. Pauline had assured the court that she only toured for a month out of the year and that she arranged for a nanny to go with her.

That situation had changed as soon as she won. Luke would have renewed the fight, but it had become clear the battle was distressing Zoey, who'd begun wetting the bed and losing weight. As a physician, let alone as a father, he put her health first.

Still, technically, he and Pauline shared custody. And the first two years, she really had only traveled for a couple of months. Then her schedule picked up, resulting in lengthy separations from his daughter and unsatisfactory attempts at homeschooling on Pauline's part.

A few months ago, just when Luke was ready to go back to court, she'd joined a new band and started a relationship with the lead guitarist, who didn't seem fond of children. Plus, at age seven, Zoey clearly needed stability and regular lessons.

To avoid another legal battle, they'd agreed to let Pauline's mother, who lived in the Orange County city of Fullerton, care for the little girl while her daughter went on tour. Although Luke considered this only a temporary compromise, he was glad to resume regular visitation, and made the hour-long drive from L.A. every weekend.

When he learned of Sean's good news, Luke had seized the chance to move to Brea, just a few minutes from Fullerton. Nothing was more precious than a closer relationship with his daughter, not even his dream of helping save more lives through research. Spending a year in a small-town practice was worth the sacrifice and, eventually, he'd be able to show a judge he was the more committed parent.

Now he thanked his cousin and walked to his car. A rental one mile away sounded ideal.

He wasn't sure he wanted a condo, though. A house would be better, in an area with other children, since he intended for Zoey to start spending weekends with him. He'd give this guy Oliver a call tomorrow and find out what else was available.

If Jane McKay recommended him, he had to be reliable. You could count on Jane for good advice.

He regretted their estrangement that last year of medical school, when she drew away emotionally after they made love. He'd missed her intensely, and in some ways still did. Damn, she was more appealing than ever, but he'd learned his lesson.

If he valued Jane McKay as a friend, and he truly did,

he'd better respect her boundaries. Besides, his effort to grow closer to his daughter took first priority.

ON A SATURDAY two weeks later, Jane set out for a walk with her mixed-breed spaniel, Stopgap. She'd picked that name because she'd imagined the pooch as a fill-in friend until she married and had children. After that, she'd vaguely pictured him shepherding her kids like Nana, the dog in *Peter Pan*.

He'd been with her nearly four years. Maybe she should have named him Everlasting. He'd certainly outstayed all the men she'd dated, none of whom came close to winning her heart. As for the kind of spark she'd felt with Luke, she still hoped to find that in a man who loved small-town life and didn't instinctively flirt with half the human race. The female half.

The golden-brown dog, whose head reached Jane's thigh, had a wavy coat and a white chest and belly that he loved for her—or anyone—to scratch. She'd read that spaniels were protective of their owners, but Stopgap must have skipped obedience school the day they taught that lesson, because he was way too eager to please everyone.

She regretted that her long hours left him alone so much, although she arranged for neighbors to walk him occasionally. But on Saturday mornings, he deserved, and received, her undivided attention.

Now he tugged at his leash as Jane, clad in a jogging suit, strolled around horseshoe-shaped Harmony Road. The arc of houses whose architecture blended Mediterranean and Spanish influences formed the core of the larger Harmony Circle development.

At the lower curve of the street a pair of 1930s cottages predated the rest of the structures. One of the Craftsman-style bungalows was next door to Jane's property, but seemed farther away due to its double-wide lot and profuse plantings, including a couple of squatty palm trees and several tall bird-of-paradise plants.

Since it had stood empty for several months, she was surprised this morning to spot a cardboard box on the porch. Perhaps the owner, Sherry Montoya, planned to sell the place and was clearing it out.

In front of the second cottage, Stopgap paused to sniff a bed of pansies. Several doors farther, artful white-on-white floral plantings testified to the talents of resident garden guru Bart Ryan. The owner of Number 15, he earned good money as a landscape consultant but helped Jane and several other neighbors plan their small gardens free of charge.

This whole neighborhood had become a beloved substitute family. An only child who'd lost both parents, Jane treasured these people, along with her coworkers. She celebrated each wedding and birthday wholeheartedly.

Her thoughts drifted to yesterday's farewell party for Sean. He'd been so excited about his upcoming adventure that the staff members had done their best to hide how much they were going to miss him. As a goodbye gift, they'd chipped in to buy several boxes of medical supplies for his new patients.

She wondered how the experience in Central America would affect Sean's buoyant optimism. He'd already done some volunteer work abroad, yet how could anyone be completely prepared for what might lie ahead?

She only hoped he'd be able to cope with any hardships and find compensation in the lives he would surely save.

Luke shared some of the same idealism, she supposed, considering his dedication to research. She wondered again why he'd decided to take over Sean's position. Surely he hadn't done it purely out of consideration for his cousin.

He'd missed the party due to obligations at his old job. Jane hadn't seen him since the day of Sean's big announcement, although they'd exchanged e-mails about such practical matters as on-call scheduling for nights and weekends. Messages that were succinct and professional in tone.

Alternately tugging Stopgap and being pulled by him, Jane continued up the far side of the U-shaped street to Crestridge Road. Several joggers, their faces familiar from the community's monthly potlucks, exchanged waves or nods with her. A teenage boy on a skateboard zoomed by, apparently lost in the music from his digital player.

She and the dog ambled along the meandering streets, past the clubhouse and swimming pool. At the small playground, a mother and toddler mounted a ladder onto the slide. Jane watched the mom, a patient of hers, sit embracing the little boy for a short, laughter-filled journey to the ground.

"Dr. McKay!" the woman called. "Look how much he's grown."

"He sure has." She'd seen that boy being born two years ago. How wonderful to be able to watch some of the babies she delivered grow up. If she worked in a major medical center, she'd miss that kind of connection.

"How'd you like to go down the slide?" Jane joked to Stopgap.

He panted up at her, ready for anything. Well, almost anything. Wiser judgment prevailing, they strolled on.

They returned to Harmony Road at the opposite, upper end. As they walked back down, each house felt intimately familiar, with a story as well-known to her as a favorite TV series. A number of the women had become Jane's friends and, dubbing themselves the Foxes, met for monthly dinners.

Jane's spirits lifted as she spotted her next-door neighbor, twenty-six-year-old Brooke Armstrong, sitting on a chaise longue with her baby daughter on a blanket beside her. How like Brooke to paint her nails in the front yard so she could socialize with whoever wandered by. And at five months, little Marlene, Jane's goddaughter, had become an adorable carbon copy of her mom, right down to the cinnamon-colored pigtails.

Neither showed any sign of alarm as Stopgap loped toward them. Gently, the dog sniffed the baby's tummy, drawing a giggle.

"I swear, that pooch thinks Marly's her puppy." Brooke indicated an empty folding chair.

"Stopgap's a boy." Jane set down the leash and accepted the seat. Her dog wouldn't stray with such enticing friends around. "You must have noticed his anatomy."

"Guess so. I wasn't thinking." Brooke blew on her nails. "What've you been up to?"

"I'd rather hear about *you*."

"You mean you'd rather hear about Marlene," her friend teased. "*My* life is boring."

Jane had to admit that her goddaughter's development entranced her. "It doesn't sound boring to me. Watching her change all the time must be fascinating. What's the latest?"

"Well, she's been doing *that* a lot." Brooke waved scarlet-tipped fingers at the baby, who had rolled over and was pushing herself up in an apparent attempt to crawl. "The kid can't wait to run me ragged. I'm thinking of attaching a lead weight as soon as she starts walking." She chuckled.

"Yeah, right." Despite the mock threat, Jane had never seen a more doting mother. "She's growing fast."

"She should, the way she eats. I've been mashing peas and bananas for her. I am *not* feeding my baby prepared food." Brooke loved cooking healthy meals for herself and Oliver, a former fast-food addict. "Of course I'm still nursing her, too."

"Good for you." Jane and Sean encouraged their maternity patients to breast-feed, since it increased babies' immunities and was better for their health in the long term. She hoped Luke held similar views.

"Speaking of babies, don't keep me in suspense." Brooke blew on her nails. "Are you going to go ahead and have one or what?"

Jane almost regretted telling her close friend that she was considering artificial insemination. Being around Marly, they naturally chatted about motherhood, and her idea had slipped out. "I'm still thinking about it."

"Your birthday's when—next week? You seemed to regard that as a kind of deadline."

"It's not for three weeks." Still, the end of March was approaching far too rapidly for Jane's taste. "Anyway, it's not as if you prick your finger on a spinning wheel on your thirty-fifth birthday and fall into a pit of infertility."

"Quit rationalizing," Brooke scolded. "Go after what you want. In case you didn't know, Maryam Hughes is reopening her home day-care center now that her mother's recovered from her stroke and gone back to work. So when you have your baby, you can take her right down the street."

"I'm glad to hear that."

"And you could leave her—or him—with me at night when you're on call," Brooke continued. "So there's nothing to stop you."

Nothing except her profoundly mixed feelings. Easy-going Brooke, who let the future take care of itself, had never been able to understand Jane's worrywart side.

She changed the subject. "There's a box outside Sherry's cottage. Has she listed it for sale?"

"Oliver says she decided to rent it." Brooke poked at one fingernail and wrinkled her nose at the mark. "Darn! This stuff's supposed to dry in ten minutes."

Maybe the box belonged to someone moving in, Jane reflected. "Did she find a tenant already?"

"Oliver referred someone to her. He didn't give me any details."

Jane was wondering what kind of new neighbors she might have, when Stopgap wandered over and nosed her arm, indicating he was ready to move on. She said goodbye and let him lead her away.

Changes in the neighborhood always intrigued her, and the cottage lay right next door. Later, once she was certain someone had indeed moved in, she'd stop by and introduce herself.

As Jane and the dog reached her house, a change in the breeze brought a whiff of smoke. She paused, concerned, although wildfires in February were rare.

After a moment, she decided the scent came from either the nearby cottage or the brush around it. She started to pull out her cell phone, but hesitated. How embarrassing if she called the fire department and it turned out her new neighbors were barbecuing.

After putting Stopgap inside her house, she hurried past the shrubbery until she caught a clear view of the cottage. No flames leaped through the roof, but the burnt odor grew stronger, possibly wafting from an open window.

And that meant someone was home. Jane had to make sure everything was all right. She hurried up the porch steps and knocked sharply.

The floor creaked, and the door swung inward.

Luke Van Dam stood there, his hair tousled and his muscular chest bare above tight jeans. His obvious confusion mirrored Jane's.

Her heart rate sped up. What on earth was Brea's newest hunk doing in the house next to hers?

Chapter Three

Luke had figured he could get away with experimenting in the kitchen and no one would find out if he screwed up. Despite his embarrassment over burning the pancakes, the sight of Jane on his doorstep gave him a jolt of pleasure.

Exertion had brightened her face, and a pink jogging suit softened the lines of her long, athletic body. She seemed less frosty than in her white coat, more the spontaneous, exuberant woman he'd known when they were younger.

He certainly hadn't expected such a warm welcome. In fact, he'd been a bit concerned that she might keep him at arm's length indefinitely. She must be an early riser, to have driven over here to wish him well in his new home. Perhaps this place lay en route from wherever she lived to her health club.

"Well, good morning," Luke said. "Welcome to chez Van Dam."

Her brown eyes narrowed. "Is everything all right?"

That puzzled him. "Why wouldn't it be?"

She waved a hand to disperse a trace of smoke. "I thought the house was on fire."

"Oh, that. Sorry if I alarmed you." He stood back to let her in. "I wasn't aware pancakes had to be watched every second." He'd only left them to move a load of laundry into the dryer.

"Did they actually catch fire?"

"No, but I'll have to reimburse my landlady for the pan. It's scorched." He'd run water over the charred mess to cool it, and tossed it in the trash.

"I'm glad you're all right." She gazed at him with wide brown eyes.

Luke's fingers itched to touch her—just on the shoulder, in a friendly manner. But that didn't seem a wise way to start their new relationship as medical partners. Instead, sharply aware of his shirtless state, he pulled on a light jacket he'd thrown over the back of a chair last night.

"It wasn't a big deal." As he led her into the cheerfully decorated kitchen, Luke glanced at the clock. Eight-thirty on a Saturday morning really was early for a social call. "There's coffee. I didn't manage to burn that."

"Thanks. I could use some."

"It's straight coffee—no fancy flavorings. Just the way you like it." He grinned. "In fact, I seem to recall you once claimed to like coffee out of a vending machine."

She ducked her head. "Did I really?"

"Maybe you were merely being polite."

"To a vending machine?"

"To me. I bought you that cup of coffee," he reminded her.

She blinked. "I'm afraid I don't recall that."

"First year. First study session." They'd had anatomy and biochemistry classes together. "You were the one who suggested a group of us join forces, remember?"

"That's because I was scared to death, the kid from Ohio brand-new in L.A.," she admitted. "I figured the rest of you would save my bacon."

"Instead, you kept us on track. You were quite a slave driver, lucky for me." He fetched a pair of mugs from the cabinet. "I was kind of distracted until we hit third year and began rotations." That was when they'd started interacting with patients on a regular basis. Dealing with real cases had inspired Luke.

"Me, too. That first year, I was in full panic mode," Jane said. "By the time I figured out that I was just as smart as the rest of you, I'd already established myself as the mother hen."

More like a cute chick than a hen. Determined not to stray into touchy territory, Luke busied himself pouring the coffee. "Was I supposed to be at the office today?"

"No. We usually close on Saturdays." From a china canister on the counter, she plucked a couple of sweetener packets. He hadn't noticed until now that his landlady had left the containers filled.

"Okay, I give up," he said.

"I'm sorry?" She regarded him quizzically.

"Is this a personal visit?" Luke asked. "I mean, I'm glad to see you. More than glad. But…"

She eyed him as if he were speaking an alien language. "But?"

"I can't help wondering why you're here."

It was her turn to look baffled. "Like I said, I thought your house was on fire."

Outside, a girl zoomed by on roller skates. When Luke peered between the flowered curtains, he was surprised to see the curb unobstructed. "Where's your car?"

"In my garage." She frowned as if *he* were the one talking in riddles.

"How'd you get here?"

She gestured toward her jogging shoes. Good heavens, had the woman run halfway across Brea to rescue him from charred pancakes?

"Exactly how far away were you when you smelled smoke?" he asked.

"I was just…" Her mouth formed an O. "I thought you knew."

"Knew what?"

"I live next door." She pointed toward the palm trees. "Oliver didn't mention it?"

"No." He hadn't discussed the neighbors with the Realtor.

How unexpected that she lived so close. And how terrific, if she were willing to move past the old awkwardness between them. Luke got along with people easily, like the colleagues he'd played tennis with in L.A., but he formed few close bonds. He could do with a friend. "Hope you don't mind my answering the door half-naked."

"Nothing I haven't seen before." Jane blushed. "Forget I said that."

"Already forgotten."

Her coffee cup clinked as she set it on the counter. "I'd better go."

"Wait." Reaching out, he caught her elbow. "I, uh…" *Think fast.* Anything to keep her from leaving on a sour note. "Hey, if you could identify this object, it would ease my mind. You know how stupid little things can drive you nuts? Kind of like seeing a familiar actor on TV and not being able to place where you know him from."

From a drawer, he fetched a man-shaped metal frame roughly six inches high. "It's kind of large to be a cookie cutter." He really *was* curious. Also, when he brought Zoey here, he wanted to be able to answer all her questions. No reason for Daddy to look any more clueless than he had to.

"It's for cutting gingerbread men," Jane answered. "Sherry loves baking the stuff. In fact, she had a gingerbread house at her wedding."

"Instead of cake?"

"There was cake, too." She picked up the coffee cup and took another sip. Apparently he hadn't driven her off, after all.

It surprised Luke that she still seemed sensitive about their long-ago encounter. He'd never been certain exactly what he'd done to make her pull back so abruptly. Something stupid he'd said, probably. He'd been an idiot in those days. He fiddled with the gingerbread cutter. "Since we're neighbors, I wonder if I might ask a favor."

"Shoot." Reaching over, Jane plucked the device from his fingers. "You'll bend that if you're not careful."

Had she felt that warmth when their hands touched? She showed no sign of it.

"Exactly my point. I'm hopeless in a kitchen," Luke said. "Would you be willing to swap cooking lessons for whatever chores I can help you with?"

He wanted to make this a second home for Zoey. And perhaps in the not-too-distant future, a full-time home.

Right now, their relationship was stuck in visiting-dad mode, with Luke bending over backward trying to entertain her when they were together. It wasn't working out too well.

A few weeks ago, he'd taken her to the beach. When the weather turned chilly, they'd shivered through a picnic of take-out fried chicken and an abbreviated session of digging in the sand. Last Saturday at the Knott's Berry Farm amusement park, they'd gone on rides until Zoey fell asleep against his shoulder.

He and his daughter needed time to simply become a family. Renting this cottage gave Luke the chance to become the kind of single dad he'd always intended to be. Part of that was learning how to cook.

"Cooking isn't rocket science." Jane bestowed on him one of those exasperated smiles he remembered from their studying days, when he used to confuse the similar-sounding names of medications. Later, when he had patients depending on him, Luke had come up with memory tricks to help him keep them straight, and double-checked every prescription. "It shouldn't be hard for a guy who performs surgery."

"People don't teach themselves to be surgeons," Luke pointed out. "They practice under an expert's guidance."

"Hmm," she said.

"Is that 'hmm' as in 'yes'?" he asked hopefully.

"That's 'hmm' as in I do need a bit of muscle in the garden." Jane eyed his biceps. "How are you with a shovel?"

His chest tightened at the directness of her gaze. "We'll find out. I could use the exercise." At Sean's suggestion, he'd joined the health club at the Brea Community Center, but he'd be happy to skip a session to get down and dirty with Jane's plants.

"It's a deal." She set her cup in the sink. "We can have our first cooking lesson next Saturday morning, if that's all right. The monthly Harmony Circle potluck's at noon. I could help you fix something to bring."

"Sounds great." Luke didn't have plans with Zoey that day, since his ex-wife would be in Fullerton and wanted their daughter to herself. "How about cookies?"

"Good enough," she agreed. "Your assignment is to find a recipe on the Internet and buy the ingredients. If you're serious about learning to cook, refrigerated dough is a no-no."

That suited him. He'd love to show Zoey how to bake cookies from scratch. "I'm on board."

She glanced toward the pan jutting from his trash can. "You might be able to save that. Pour on a thick layer of baking soda and sprinkle it with a little water. Let it soak and then scrub."

"I'll try that."

Her cell phone rang, and she whipped it out. "Dr. McKay… Sure thing. I'll be there in ten minutes." She pocketed the phone.

"Patient in labor?"

She nodded. "See you Monday."

"I'll try not to burn anything in the meantime."

"Good idea."

As she strode out, Luke wished he'd had time to tell her about his daughter. He could certainly use her advice about Zoey.

How interesting that Jane had worked as a nanny. He'd like to know more of her history, and more about the kind of person she'd become. When he learned that she and Sean were buying a practice together, Luke had thought about getting back in touch, but by then he'd been married.

At least she'd agreed to a cooking lesson, and a resumption, at some level, of their friendship. Right next door. Wasn't that a stroke of good luck? he mused, and went to look for baking soda.

WHY WAS LUKE SO KEEN on cooking? Jane wondered as she hurried home. And why the curiosity about the gingerbread cutter? He'd changed—and she sensed there was a story there, if only he'd tell her.

Out of curiosity, she'd dropped a few questions to Sean regarding Luke's activities these past few years. He'd mentioned a divorce, but proved unusually reticent about revealing more. "You should ask Luke," he'd said.

A divorce. Much as she regretted hearing that the man's marriage had fallen apart, Jane couldn't claim to be surprised. Of course, she had no idea what had happened between him and his wife. Still, Luke had never struck her as the type most likely to celebrate a fiftieth anniversary.

The man had a brilliant mind and a gift for surgery, but he'd let flirtations distract him from studying as hard as he should have. Girlfriends flocked to him like iron filings to a magnet. Luke genuinely liked women, and he'd never been deliberately cruel, but several times, Jane had comforted fellow med students and nurses who were bewildered when Luke ended their affairs as casually as if he were returning a library book.

"He doesn't have a clue how much he hurt me," one young woman had wailed. "It's like he thinks I'm some friend he plays basketball with, and now he's tired of basketball."

Despite everything she'd known, Jane, too, had succumbed. Chalk it up to the effects of close contact, to a long-simmering attraction, to a lowered guard late at night. Once she'd allowed herself to kiss him—she still didn't remember who'd made the first move, or perhaps they'd both moved simultaneously—she'd been powerless to stop. No, not powerless, eager to continue. She flinched at the memory of wrapping herself around Luke as they fell across his bed. Even now, her body quivered at the thought.

She'd recognized her mistake as soon as the heat of their passion faded. She'd lain there in his arms, longing to hear him say he loved her and feeling like an utter fool for entrusting her heart to Luke, of all men. Naturally, he'd said nothing of the kind, merely murmured that he'd like to do this again sometime.

She'd left vowing to pretend the whole thing never happened. But for the rest of their fourth year, she'd avoided being alone with him, and he'd never pressed her to continue the affair. All he'd done was look hurt and confused.

Now, Luke exerted the same captivating charm as always. Jane marched into her house, irritated with herself for noticing and for agreeing to spend time with him away from work. On the other hand, why should she care?

She would never be naive enough to fall under his spell again. That infatuation lay in the past, and she intended to keep it there.

ON SUNDAY, Luke took Zoey to Disneyland in nearby Anaheim. They had so much fun on the rides, they stayed much later than he'd planned.

He hauled his tired, cranky daughter back to her grandmother's, and received what he had to admit was a well-deserved tongue-lashing for keeping her out so late on a school night. If the dark circles beneath his daughter's blue eyes hadn't been reproach enough, her grandmother's labored breathing made him regret inconveniencing her. At sixty-seven, Hetty was overweight and suffered from diabetes.

Luke had tried to give her advice more than once about eating more healthily and the need for exercise. Hetty always agreed to try, but nothing changed. At his urging, she *had* consulted a physician and begun taking medication, but pills couldn't entirely undo the effect of her unhealthy lifestyle.

After apologizing, Luke asked, "Is it okay if I take her out next Sunday?" Although Pauline had e-mailed him to say that she'd be visiting her mother and daughter on Friday and part of Saturday, she planned to rejoin the band that evening.

"I wouldn't count on it," Hetty grumbled.

Her comment surprised him. "Why not?"

"I need to talk to my daughter first. Then I'll let you know." That sounded ominous, but the tightness of her expression put him off asking more.

Luke reminded himself that, since he had joint custody, no one could prevent him from seeing Zoey. Whatever the problem was, they'd work it out. "I'll call you Sunday around noon."

"That would be fine."

He didn't have time to think much about the coming weekend during that hectic first few days working in Brea. There were new office procedures to master, case histories to review, patients to meet and the staff's personalities to become familiar with.

On Tuesday and Thursday mornings, Luke performed the surgeries Sean had scheduled, and during his Thursday-night on-call shift, he delivered four babies. Thank goodness he and Jane shared off-hours duty with another obstetrical practice, or they'd have been working nonstop.

All the same, he wished he didn't have to give up his weekly visits to a low-cost L.A. clinic for pregnant teens. It was too far to drive now and he wanted to spend more time with Zoey. A tennis-playing colleague had talked him into volunteering, and Luke was grateful. Helping impoverished young women, many of them victims of abuse or neglect, had given him a strong sense of purpose and helped ease the loneliness during Zoey's absences.

He'd promised to keep in touch with one of his patients whom he was mentoring, so it came as no surprise when his phone rang on Saturday morning and the display read "Annie Raft." The eighteen-year-old with a zany sense of humor and a heart-tugging child-like quality had arrived at the clinic six months pregnant, the baby's father long gone. A month later, when she became homeless after a fight with her mother, Luke had arranged for a social worker to find her somewhere to live, and had scheduled extra time to listen to and encourage her.

After delivering her little girl, he'd gone with a clinic volunteer to visit her several times. Annie had loved the way he played with baby Tina, tickling her and inventing games as he'd done for Zoey.

"You're like the dad I never knew," she'd said wistfully. "I mean, like the dad I wished I'd had."

When he'd told her he was moving to Orange County, she'd burst into tears. Luke had assured her she could call him to chat, and had given her his cell-phone number.

He supposed some people might think he was too involved, but he'd grown to care about this girl. Fortunately, she'd recently found a new boyfriend, a firefighter with a steady job and an upbeat temperament. When Luke took them and the baby out for dinner before his move, he'd been impressed with the young man's obvious affection for both Annie and Tina. It seemed that she'd found a safe haven at last.

"Hi, Annie," Luke said into the phone. "I enjoyed your last e-mail."

"The doctor jokes? I thought you'd like them," she said.

"How're you doing?"

"Great! Brian and I are going to move in together," she announced. "I want you to be the first to know. Well, aside from my roommate. I had to tell *her,* of course."

"Congratulations." Luke would have preferred to hear about wedding plans, but perhaps this was a first step.

"We're apartment hunting," she said. "Oh, here's Tina! Listen." After some offstage coaxing, the baby babbled a few syllables into the receiver.

Her sweet voice ricocheted through Luke. *Just like Zoey's used to do.*

"She's amazing," he told the proud mother.

"Yeah!" Annie crowed. "Oh, hey, gotta go. Brian's here early. We'll have you over for dinner when we move in."

"I'd love that."

When he clicked off, Luke noticed the time on the

phone read 9:22 a.m. Jane had agreed to stop by at nine for their cooking session. How unusual for her to run late.

He pressed her number in his cell phone, but the call didn't go through. She must either be on the phone or out of range. Well, she *did* live next door, a fact that increased his options significantly.

Interrupting her might not be the most diplomatic tactic. But she had promised.

Luke went outside and strolled past the palm trees to the adjacent lot. He'd glimpsed Jane's two-story house from his car, but, up close, he paused to admire the profusion of flowers in the tiled front planter. What a merry blend of colors, all carefully tended and, as far as he could tell, weed-free. How like Jane to be both spirited and precise.

He was about to ring the bell when the sound of her voice floated from an open upstairs window. "No, I haven't made an appointment, Brooke. Getting inseminated is a major step."

Inseminated? He hadn't meant to eavesdrop on such a personal conversation.

"Please don't mention it to the foxes." He wondered what she meant by "foxes." Maybe he'd misunderstood the word. "What am I supposed to tell them? Hi, my name is Jane and I'm a baby-aholic?"

The discovery that she wanted a baby startled Luke. Jane always seemed so self-contained that, if he'd thought about it at all, he'd have figured she had too much sense to run herself ragged between a career and single parenthood. Still, he had enough experience to understand the strength of the parental drive.

But having a child alone was far from an ideal situation. Luke had learned a lot these past years, including the fact that Zoey craved closeness with her father as well as her mother. It must be difficult for any single parent to compensate.

Well, Jane was old enough and smart enough to make choices without his advice.

Overhead, she resumed her side of the conversation. "Thanks for the encouragement. Of course I don't mind you calling me about Marlene's rash. I'll take a look at the potluck. Oh, Lord, what time is it?"

That was his cue to sneak home undetected, Luke decided. She'd never suspect he'd heard a thing.

Except that, as he turned to go, her sprinklers whirred into action. His instinctive curse and flying leap onto the porch brought an eruption of barking from inside. He couldn't have raised more racket if he'd set off a burglar alarm.

"Who's there?" demanded Jane's voice from upstairs.

"It's me," he responded sheepishly.

"Would that be Salesman Me, Peeping Tom Me or Dr. Me?" she inquired.

"Dr. Me."

"Wait there."

A minute later, the water shut off. He tried flapping his shirt to dry it, which proved about as effective as emptying a bathtub with a teaspoon. Thank goodness for seventy-degree weather in March.

The door opened. "Sorry about our cooking date. I'm running late." That was obvious from her rumpled hair and a short nightgown that skimmed her breasts and barely cleared her hips. What incredibly long, smooth legs. He had a sudden, vivid memory of how they'd felt, tangled up with his. "I must have turned off the alarm clock in my sleep."

Luke took a deep breath and hoped she didn't notice the telltale bulge in his jeans. "Maybe we should cancel my lesson."

Her gaze scorched across the shirt stuck to his chest. "My sprinklers were rough on you, weren't they? You look like a six-foot-tall drowned rat."

"Six foot one. And yes, you have ruthless, possibly sociopathic sprinklers."

She laughed. "Did you buy ingredients already?"

"I did," Luke said. "You're the one who taught me to come to class prepared."

"Bring everything over and we'll cook here," she offered. "I have to fix a pasta salad and that's going to take a while, but I did promise to help you."

"Thanks. I'll go change." Luke made his getaway. The image of her in that close-fitting silk teddy stuck in his mind all the way home.

While she'd been merely pretty in medical school, she'd matured into an alluring woman. And she hadn't seemed the least bit shy about letting him see her that way.

But Jane was his new partner. He didn't intend to risk their business relationship or their tentatively resumed friendship by moving too fast.

That didn't mean he couldn't think about the possibilities.

Chapter Four

After setting a pot of water on the stove to boil, Jane ran upstairs to throw on some clothes. Stopgap loped behind, complaining in his doggy way about the disruptions to his schedule.

"Don't blame Luke," she told him. "We did have a date of sorts. And I'm sorry about missing your walk this morning. I'll make up for it tomorrow."

With a whine, he flopped onto the bathroom floor. She pushed aside a twinge of guilt.

As she shrugged out of her teddy, Jane recalled the heat that had rushed through her as she caught Luke's gaze trailing across her body. Did he think she hadn't noticed? How could any woman fail to spot that?

She wasn't sure why she hadn't grabbed her robe. Perhaps because Luke had acted so casual the other day when she'd seen him bare chested. It wouldn't hurt him to get teased a little in exchange. Besides, it felt good to be appreciated by a sexy man, even though there was no way they were going to take things any further.

A short while later, Jane was trimming broccoli and

sugar snap peas when the doorbell rang. She hurried to let Luke in.

Above a tray piled with baking supplies, a deep purple shirt brought out the violet depths of his eyes. She was glad she'd put on tailored slacks and a figure-hugging top instead of her usual weekend odds and ends.

Okay, now *she* was staring at *him*. His appreciative smile told her he hadn't missed a thing. "You look great. But I prefer that sleek little number you were wearing before."

"So do I."

"Whoa!" His brows lifted. "Care to explain?"

"It's very comfortable," Jane deadpanned. "Now let's get to work. I am *not* baking those cookies for you."

"No one asked you to."

"Point taken."

He seemed to fill her tiny black-and-white-tiled kitchen. "There's nothing like a little good-natured badinage to get the juices flowing on a Saturday morning."

"Bad in what?" she shot back. That sounded like a medical procedure, although she was pretty sure it wasn't.

"It means repartee. My dad used to make us memorize a new word every day."

From the pantry, Jane retrieved a package of rotini noodles and a can of olives. "My dad was a truck driver. He taught me a new curse word a day." That was only a slight exaggeration.

Luke chuckled. "I'll bet those are more useful than 'badinage.'"

"Depends on whom you want to impress." She glanced at the recipe he'd brought and told him to set the oven to 375 degrees. "Is your dad an English teacher?" she asked, fetching a mixing bowl for him.

"He's a retired financial consultant."

"Don't you have a couple of brothers, too?" She vaguely recalled him mentioning them, but she'd forgotten most of what he'd said about his family.

"One's a lawyer. The other's a financial guru like Dad. And you're an only child, right?"

"Yep." Well, they'd covered that topic. Now to the matter at hand. She showed how to soften the butter and mix the dough, and watched to make sure he didn't drop any eggshell into the bowl.

He had strong, sure hands, the hands of a surgeon. While Jane had outshone Luke at diagnosing and prescribing, he'd proved a natural in the operating room. He knew just how to touch a woman, too, she recalled, and set to chopping vegetables with more vigor than was really necessary.

Following her directions, Luke folded in the chocolate chips smoothly. "What're you making?"

Jane showed him the pasta salad recipe and explained that she had to cook the noodles, steam the vegetables, make the dressing then mix it and let the whole thing chill. "I should have done this hours ago. I doubt it'll be ready by noon."

"Surely everyone doesn't arrive right on time."

She had to admit he was right. "Okay, I'll quit obsessing."

He paused, wrist-deep in dough. "You keep grinning at me."

"I do?" He looked cute in a kitchen, she realized, embarrassed at having been caught. It was just that she'd never associated Luke with anything remotely domestic.

"I figured I must have a chocolate chip stuck to my nose or something."

"Sure. Give it a dab and knock it off."

He reached for his nose, and wound up with a smear of dough on one cheek. "Hey! Dirty trick!"

"Which you fell for. Sucker!" Amused, Jane dampened a paper towel and wiped his face. "I can't imagine how you maintain a sterile surgical field when you're so clumsy." Even though, of course, he was nothing of the sort.

He grinned. "If my ego ever gets too big, I can rely on good old Jane to bring it down to size."

"Is that who I am? Good old Jane?" No sooner had she uttered those words than she regretted them. "Don't mind me."

"Maybe we should get this out in the open," he said quietly. "I mean, about what happened between us."

How about what's happening now? Like the tautness of her breasts and the longing to hold him... *Don't think about it.* "That's old news," she said with feigned lightness, and grabbed a baking sheet. "Let me show you how to grease this. The recipe says not to, but don't believe everything you read."

Instead of responding, he stood there regarding her with an expression that was hard to figure out. Why couldn't she guess what he was thinking? In med school, she'd practically been able to read his mind.

But they weren't in school anymore. Jane thrust a spray bottle of oil into Luke's hand and watched while he used it.

"I take it the past is verboten?" he asked.

"Is that another of your posh words?" she teased.

"Right up there with *gesundheit*."

She showed him how to drop rounded tablespoonfuls of dough onto the sheet, then let him take over. "Very neatly spaced, Doc."

"Thanks for being such a good teacher," he said. "You're going to make a great mom."

"What?"

He blinked. "I mean, someday."

He hadn't sounded as if he meant someday. Oh, good heavens, he'd been standing right below her bedroom. And she'd been talking much louder than she should have near an open window. "You heard me on the phone."

He ducked his head. "Sorry. I didn't mean to eavesdrop."

Of all the people she'd rather not find out about her private yearnings, Luke headed the list. As her office partner, however, he'd be bound to learn the truth if she chose to go ahead with this. Not that she would ever in a million years let him deliver *her* baby.

"It's just an option. I haven't made up my mind." Turning back to her work, Jane tried to keep her tone casual.

"You're not my patient, so it's not my place to comment." After spooning out the last of the dough, Luke slid the baking sheet into the oven. It got stuck at an angle, but he straightened it and closed the door.

"What do you mean, comment?" When it came to medical issues, Jane knew as much as he did. "About what?"

"Parenthood." He set his watch alarm for what she presumed was the correct time: ten minutes.

Parenthood? "And you're an expert on that?" On the other hand, she'd rather let him say his piece and get it over with. "Go ahead. Give me your sage advice."

Luke washed his hands in the sink, scrubbing the nails as if prepping for surgery. "Kids are demanding and complicated. It's hard for a single parent to meet all their needs."

Jane dumped the pasta into the strainer with such force that hot water splashed onto the counter. "I never took you for the judgmental type."

"Heck, it's hard for *two* parents to cope. Besides, you asked for my opinion."

"All right. Now you've aired it, and we're done."

"You never intended to listen, did you?" he challenged.

Jane recognized she might be overreacting, and didn't care. "I don't have to justify myself to you."

"No, you don't," Luke agreed. "But fathers aren't superfluous. I presume you've read the studies."

She had. Children who lacked fathers ran a higher risk of getting into trouble as adolescents. "Statistics don't tell the whole story."

"True." He raised his hands, palms out. "I've said all I mean to say, and I'll shut up. Peace?"

"Peace." Tight-lipped, Jane carried on with her salad, while he washed his mixing bowl and utensils. She didn't need to be reminded that she'd be better off if she'd found a wonderful guy the way Brooke and some of her other friends had.

When his watch alarm went off, Luke removed the perfectly browned cookies.

He broke the silence at last. "Listen, I didn't mean to offend you. I thought we were just having a discussion."

"A *personal* discussion provoked by your eavesdropping." Why couldn't he offer support rather than criticism as she weighed this major decision?

Luke transferred the cookies to a heavy paper plate. "Maybe I should explain about the single-parenting thing."

"No, you shouldn't."

"I'm not simply offering an opinion. I've been meaning to tell you…" He broke off as Stopgap padded into the kitchen. Flopping onto Jane's feet, the dog rolled over and waved his paws in the air. "What's he doing?"

"We missed our morning walk." Suddenly she itched for the release of a brisk stroll, with only the dog for company. Besides, she was in no mood for more high-handed advice. "Why don't I meet you at the potluck?"

"Are you angry?" Luke asked.

"I'm furious."

"You shouldn't be."

"You are the most aggravating…"

"I believe the correct word is *irritating*."

"That, too!"

He covered the plate with plastic wrap. "See you at the potluck."

"See you." Thank goodness there'd be plenty of other people around. Jane really didn't want to waste her pasta salad by dumping it over this man's arrogant head.

After Luke left, she cleaned up, refrigerated the salad and attached Stopgap's leash. Outside, she stalked up the street, her anger dissipating slowly as she replayed Luke's remarks.

For some reason, his opinion mattered to her. And that fact bugged her more than anything.

LUKE WAS SPRAWLED on the couch with a medical journal, staring at an article about the latest developments in 3-D mammograms and not absorbing a word of it.

Why was Jane so eager to have a child by herself? Surely plenty of men would love to… No, that wasn't right. A woman didn't need plenty of men. Just the right one. Obviously, she'd never found him.

It certainly wasn't Luke. She'd made that clear ten years ago, beating a retreat from his apartment as if he carried smallpox and she hadn't been vaccinated. Not that he'd been ready for a serious relationship at that point, but he'd hoped for more. She'd never forgiven him, either. The worst of it was, he still didn't know exactly how he'd ticked her off.

Just had a gift for it, he supposed. He'd stomped all over her toes a short while ago with his clumsy remarks about parenting. He'd only been trying to share his personal experiences. Wasn't that what friends did?

The doorbell rang. His spirits lifting in the hope that she'd decided to stop by en route to the party, he hurried to answer.

Instead of Jane, Luke opened the door on the friendly face of his blond landlady, Sherry Montoya. Her tall, dark-haired husband, Rafe, stood behind her on the porch, along with his five-year-old twins, Juan and Sofia.

"Going to the potluck?" Sherry asked. "If you'd like to walk over with us, we could introduce you around."

Luke readily agreed. A few minutes later, plate of cookies in hand, he strolled along with the family.

"I love this neighborhood," Sherry enthused as they passed a house with a striped awning. "It feels like home now, even though everybody hated me when I first moved in."

It was hard to imagine anyone hating someone with Sherry's outgoing personality. "Why on earth?"

"I wanted to tear down the cottage and replace it with a huge house. Stupid idea, huh? That would have destroyed part of the neighborhood's history, not to mention its charm."

"What changed your mind?"

"The man I'd trusted, my fiancé, stole my money. I couldn't afford to rebuild," Sherry told him. "It's a long story, but the important part is that I found myself living here unexpectedly. You might call it a growing experience."

As they crossed the street, her husband reached for Juan's hand and Sherry took Sofia's. "She's a quick learner," Rafe commented. "And a fantastic mom."

"What happened to the fiancé?" Luke asked.

"The FBI finally caught up with him," Sherry said buoyantly. "I got most of my money back, too. But by then, I'd discovered there are more valuable ways to spend my life than buying designer clothes and throwing fancy parties. Unless they're for fund-raisers, of course."

"The children live with you full-time?" Catching Rafe's startled expression, Luke explained, "I figured your ex-wife probably had joint custody."

Neither of his neighbors spoke until the twins scampered ahead along the sidewalk. Then Rafe said, "Juan and Sofia are my niece and nephew. Their parents died in a fire almost two years ago."

"I'm sorry."

As they turned a corner, the murmur of voices and splash of water greeted them. Ahead, trees surrounded a pool dotted with swimmers and colorful floating tubes. On the terrace above, the doors of the glass-fronted clubhouse stood open, allowing a small crowd of people to circulate between outdoor tables and the indoor serving area.

Luke caught the scent of grilling meat. As they entered through a gate, he recognized Oliver as one of the two men flipping hamburgers at a pair of barbecues. They joined a crowd of roughly fifty people, some waiting in a line for burgers, others filling their plates at serving stations.

"I'd start with the desserts if I didn't have to set a good example for the kids," Rafe muttered, indicating a table laden with goodies. Two junior-high-age girls stood slicing cake onto paper plates, while a third tucked business cards onto each one.

Sherry indicated the trio. "That's Brittany in the frilly apron. She runs a part-time baking business. Carly, the one with highlighted hair, is Brittany's stepsister, and Suzy Ching's their friend. We've started calling them the Little Foxes."

He'd heard that term before, Luke recalled. "Foxes. Is that a women's group?"

His landlady nodded. "We're friends who meet for dinner and discussions." She wedged her potato salad onto a table. "It used to stand for Females Only—Exuberantly Single until some of us got married. Now we're just the Foxes, and never mind why."

During the next few minutes, Luke met his other

neighbors, who greeted him warmly and urged him to sample their various dishes. Friendly place. He could see why Jane liked practicing medicine in such a close-knit community.

Luke hoped Zoey wouldn't grow too attached to it, though. Once Sean returned, he intended to apply for a staff position at a teaching hospital where he could expand his expertise and help pioneer ways to save more lives. But only if he could bring his daughter along, of course.

As he filled his plate and joined the Montoyas and a couple of Sherry's friends at a table, Luke kept glancing around. It was a relief when, at last, he spotted Jane's swinging stride approaching the gate from the sidewalk.

His spirits lifted. Finally, the party could begin in earnest.

JANE GLIMPSED Luke sitting with a group on the club-house terrace, surrounded, of course, by admiring women. No wonder. He looked like a movie star, with those striking features and that brightness in his eyes…which fixed on Jane. Unbidden, a tiny thrill ran through her.

"Hey." Luke raised a hand.

She nodded and went to set down her bowl. The walk with Stopgap had worn the edge off her annoyance with him. In retrospect, he'd only been giving the kind of advice he'd probably offer to a patient, and with good reason.

The painful part, Jane supposed, was that she shared some of his reservations. Going into motherhood alone was far from ideal.

Before she could join him, however, Brooke ap-

peared with the baby. Jane inspected the rash, pro-
nounced it a mild case of diaper irritation, and told
Brooke how to treat it. By the time Jane returned from
washing her hands, Luke had finished eating and was
standing by the dessert table, surrounded by an atten-
tive group of mostly females ranging from young girls
to Minnie Ortiz, who must be pushing ninety.

He didn't flirt consciously, as far as Jane could
tell. He simply exuded masculinity combined with
natural warmth.

Too hungry to join the conversation, she took her
plate to the picnic table, now occupied only by her
model-thin friend Renée, who was nursing a diet soda.
"Your new partner is drop-dead gorgeous." The hairdresser slanted an appreciative glance at Luke.

Jane didn't want to be jealous of her friend. Or of
anyone. "Interested?"

"I wouldn't waste my time," Renée said. "In case you
didn't notice, his face lit up when he saw you."

"Which explains why he bolted from the table before
I got here," Jane tossed back.

"You always underrate yourself," Renée told her.

"Not at all." Jane felt quite comfortable with her appearance. Most of the time, anyway.

Renée regarded her assessingly. "Now that your hair's
longer, I could do something with it." She slapped her
palm on the table. "I know! I'll give you a makeover for
your birthday. That's coming up in a few weeks, right?"

"I'd be happy to pay you." Her hair *could* use reshap-
ing, and Renée had worked wonders for some of the
other Foxes.

Renée dismissed the offer with a wave of her hand.

"Not a chance. Call me at work and we'll set up an appointment."

"Thank you."

A trace of aftershave tickled Jane's nose as Luke slid onto the bench beside her. That and his body heat left her feeling quite light-headed.

He leaned toward her, his eyes widening as if in appeal. "Help. I'm in over my head here."

She took a deep breath to calm her reaction. "Help with what?"

Before he could answer, Minnie and the girls joined them, along with Alice Watson, a retired school principal who hosted the Foxes' meetings.

"We wanted to talk to you, too, Jane," Alice said. "We were asking Luke if he had any ideas about how we could preserve Harmony Circle's history."

"What do you mean?" Jane hoped she hadn't missed some new proposal to tear down houses or extend nearby Berry Street into a major thoroughfare.

Everyone started talking at once. "New people move in and they have no idea about our history," explained Minnie. "If we aren't careful, we could turn into just another faceless development."

"I love this place," said Brittany the baker. "I've lived here all my life." Jane thought that must be all of thirteen years.

"I've taken zillions of pictures," added her stepsister Carly.

"I suggested they ask a historian to get them organized," Luke said.

The talk turned to the merits and shortcomings of scrapbooks and networking sites. Everyone kept looking to Luke as if he should have the answer. He, in turn, regarded Jane pleadingly. "Any ideas?"

She longed to devise a brilliant plan, if only to impress him. Usually, Jane couldn't care less about impressing people.

"Harmony Circle already has its own Web site," she pointed out. "We could expand its function. You know, put together a digital history, with photos and reminiscences."

Luke laid a hand atop hers. "That's exactly what we need."

His use of the word *we* gave Jane the strangest little twitch of excitement. As if he already felt at home here. As if he might stay permanently.

Not that it concerned her, particularly. But the area could use another outstanding obstetrician.

Everyone seemed to love her suggestion. Carly volunteered to start by interviewing Minnie, and others tossed out more ideas. As they talked, Luke removed his hand, but the warmth remained.

Jane averted her face and hoped no one noticed the pink in her cheeks. Okay, so she did care if he stayed. Life sure had more of a zing with Luke around, even at his most maddening.

When she went to throw her empty plate in the trash, he followed. The group remained at the table, talking excitedly. "This is a great place," he said.

She dropped her soda can in a recycling bin. "You've had an impact." *And not just on those other women.*

"There's something I started to tell you about earlier but we got interrupted. Jane, I think you should know…" His cell phone rang. "Oh, great. Sometimes I'd like to throw this damn thing in the swimming pool."

"Our patients depend on them," Jane reminded him.

"If you ask me, there was a lot to be said for sending a messenger with a horse and buggy," Luke groused, and checked the display.

He wasn't on call today, Jane reflected as he put the phone to his ear. But a patient's personal physician might be consulted in an emergency, all the same.

"Yes?" As he listened, his muscles tensed. He made a few terse comments—"What do you mean?"—and, more angrily, "How the hell did that happen?"

Jane became edgy along with him. What was wrong?

"I'll be right there," he snapped at last, closing his phone.

"What's the matter?"

His jaw worked, and then he blurted, "My daughter's missing."

What daughter? With a rush of understanding, she realized that must be what he'd been trying to tell her. Luke was a parent. That might explain why he felt qualified to give advice on the subject. "What can I do?"

For a moment, as his fists clenched, she expected him to shrug her off, and then he said, "Come with me. Keep me centered or I might crash the car. Or explode."

"Absolutely." Nothing else mattered but the child who might be in danger. "Let's go."

Luke broke into a run toward the gate. Calling a quick farewell to her startled friends, Jane hurried to join him.

Chapter Five

His muscles straining with anxiety, Luke kept pressing too hard on the gas and had to force himself to ease off. Jane's presence grounded him, exactly as he'd hoped. Besides, smashing up his car on the way to Hetty's house wasn't going to do his daughter any good.

As he drove, he sketched the details of his marriage and divorce aloud. In Jane's responses, he heard no hint of judgment, either for the accidental pregnancy or for his neglecting to tell her up front that he had a daughter, even though, as his medical partner and friend, she might well be affected by his family situation. Hell, she *was* being affected.

At a red light, he extracted a photo of Zoey from his wallet. Jane studied it as they accelerated south on Harbor Boulevard toward Fullerton. "What a cutie. How old is she?"

"Seven. And impulsive. Who knows what's made her take off?" Seeing how Jane gripped the armrest, Luke gathered that they were traveling too fast and slowed down a little.

"I hate to raise such a scary issue, but are you sure she wasn't abducted?" Jane asked.

His throat tightened at the suggestion. "Pauline said she and her mother were arguing, which, apparently, upset Zoey. She ran out and they can't find her." Which didn't mean someone hadn't grabbed her later.

"That doesn't sound so bad. She probably went to a friend's house," Jane said reassuringly.

"She's new in the area, so she doesn't have many friends. They contacted everyone they could think of. Including the police, of course. She's been gone about four hours." Far too long for such a small child.

Luke pictured his daughter's elfin face and sparkling blue eyes. He couldn't bear it if anything happened to her. Why hadn't Pauline recognized the danger immediately? Why had she waited so long before alerting him?

"You look like you're about to burst a blood vessel," Jane advised. "Dial it down a notch, Doc."

He hadn't realized he was glowering. "I guess I'm angry at my ex-wife and at myself, too. If we'd given Zoey a stable home, I doubt she'd have run off."

"Based on what you've told me, I'm not sure either of you could have saved this marriage." Jane turned toward him, shifting the seat belt across her knit top. "The two of you don't sound compatible."

Luke managed a slight smile. "I guess I wasn't thinking about the long term when I dated her."

"Did you ever think about…" She broke off.

About the long term with Jane? But she'd given him no choice, simply stalked out and kept him at arm's length ever after. When he'd asked if he'd done something to offend her, she'd just shaken her head.

"We made a mistake," she'd told him. "Let's not repeat it."

Still, she'd left a question unfinished. "What were you going to ask?" Luke inquired as he turned off Harbor Boulevard into the old-fashioned neighborhood where Hetty lived.

"I don't honestly know," Jane admitted. "Random thoughts keep flitting through my brain. I'm still trying to sort out this new Luke, the caring father, from the wild-eyed medical student."

"Sleepy eyed," he corrected.

"We were all walking zombies," she agreed. Late nights and long shifts at the hospital had taken their toll.

A few streets farther, they arrived at Hetty's modest frame home. A car bearing the plates of a rental agency sat in front. Pauline's, Luke assumed.

Worry clamped around his heart as he bolted from the vehicle. Jane matched his rapid pace up the walkway.

His ex-wife opened the door before he could ring. "They haven't found her yet."

Despite her obvious worry, Pauline looked younger than her thirty years. She'd done something trendy with her blond hair, transforming it with a shaggy cut and strands of coppery red. Right now, though, he wouldn't have cared if she'd shaved herself bald.

Seeing her curious glance at his companion, he said, "This is Dr. Jane McKay, my new medical partner."

"And next-door neighbor," Jane added as the women shook hands. "I happened to be there when he got your call."

Pauline ushered them inside. "We were helping the police canvass the neighborhood but Mom started feeling ill, so we came back."

"Is she all right?" Despite his anxiety about Zoey, Luke didn't want to neglect Hetty's health.

"All she needs is rest." Pauline paced the furniture-crammed living room. A couple of children's books lay scattered where Zoey must have dropped them. "And to see her granddaughter safe."

Jane scanned the room. "Any idea what she took with her?"

"I don't see what that has to do with anything." His ex-wife stared at her.

"If she ran out empty-handed, she's less likely to go far," Jane explained. "But if she took a few things, she might have a plan. Did she have any money?"

"She's only seven!" Pauline flared, before collecting herself. More calmly she answered, "She does save part of her allowance, so she might have twenty or thirty dollars."

To Luke, Jane's inquiries opened a new realm of possibilities. "Your mother mentioned that they rode the bus to the mall a few weeks ago, which means Zoey's at least somewhat familiar with the transit system. I can't figure out where she'd head, though."

"To an old neighborhood?" Jane suggested. "She might miss her friends."

"I don't think so," Pauline said. "She doesn't have many friends."

"To the mall?" Jane persisted.

Pauline made a nervous gesture. "When Mom and I were squabbling, Zoey shouted that she wished we lived at Disneyland because then we'd be happy all the time. But that's just foolishness."

During their visit to the Magic Kingdom, Zoey *had*

said she'd like to stay forever, Luke recalled. "A bus runs straight down Harbor Boulevard to Disneyland." They'd passed it while driving home from the theme park. "There's a stop a few blocks from here."

"The driver wouldn't let a seven-year-old ride alone, would he?" Pauline protested.

"Maybe she climbed on with a group of people and he didn't notice," Jane said.

Luke's thoughts raced ahead. "In case you're right, we'd better alert the police." This could mean his daughter had covered a far greater distance than anyone had suspected.

Pauline nodded reluctantly. "It can't hurt."

"I'll check on your mother while you're doing that," Jane offered.

Luke shot her a look of gratitude. Today more than ever, he appreciated her good judgment and quick thinking. And the fact that she'd come with him. He needed someone to keep him on track.

He got on the phone to the Fullerton dispatcher, who thanked him for the tip and promised to alert Disneyland security as well as the Anaheim police. "We'll widen the search parameters immediately," she assured him.

After he hung up, Pauline stood braced defensively. "This isn't my fault."

"No one said it was." Despite his anger that she'd let this happen, Luke saw no sense starting an argument. He glanced toward Hetty's bedroom, wishing Jane would return so they could get moving.

"The band has a performance tonight in San Diego. If I cancel, we'll lose a lot of money." She swallowed hard. "Jason doesn't understand about kids. I mean, he's not used to them."

"Then let me take her, like I've always wanted."

"We agreed she should stay with my mother!"

"I said yes because the court forced me to," Luke snapped, abandoning his earlier resolve to keep calm. "Now she's missing. What were you and Hetty arguing about that upset her?"

"Nothing we can't work out."

Jane emerged from the hall and nodded at Pauline. "Your mom's vital signs are stable. Her medication made her sleepy, which, in view of the stress she's under, might be a good thing. Is there anyone you could call to stay with her for a few days?"

"My aunt Bea." Pauline seemed to perk up at the idea. "She's said she'd fly out if Mom ever needed her."

"Good idea." Jane glanced at Luke.

Now that he knew Hetty was all right, the last of his patience crumbled. "Let's head out."

"There's a park a few blocks over," his ex-wife interjected. "You should check there on the way."

He'd intended to head straight for Anaheim. "Haven't the police already searched it?"

Pauline twisted her hands together. "Yes, but she might hide from them."

He stopped in midstride. "Why?"

Her chin lifted defiantly. "After a performance, musicians like to let off steam. My last band occasionally got a little rowdy at the motel."

"Rowdy enough for someone to call the police?" Luke demanded, dismayed by this latest disclosure.

"Only once and no one got arrested. Besides, I'm not

with that group anymore. But when the police showed up, I told her to hide because I was afraid things might get rough."

Thanks to Pauline's irresponsible bandmates, Zoey feared the police. Luke could scarcely believe she'd put their daughter in such danger.

Jane edged toward the door. "We should go look for Zoey."

Trust her to keep their priorities straight. "You're right." Avoiding Pauline's gaze so he wouldn't be tempted to lash out at her again, Luke stalked out.

He was going to find his daughter. And then he meant to keep her.

JANE HAD NEVER SEEN Luke this upset, she reflected as they drove toward the park. Much as she hated to share more bad news, he deserved to see the whole picture. "Did you know Pauline's mother has a heart condition?"

"What?" Luke tore his anguished gaze from the road. "How do you know that?"

"I saw the pill bottles on her bedside table." Jane had recognized the medication immediately.

He cruised toward a small neighborhood park where the children swarmed the playground equipment. "I knew she had diabetes, but not that."

Heart disease was a frequent complication of diabetes, so the two illnesses might be related. "Taking care of a child must be hard on her," Jane mused.

"Pauline shouldn't have imposed on her. I only went along with it as a temporary measure." He was pulling into a parking spot when his phone rang. He tapped a button so he could listen hands-free. "Yes?"

Jane swallowed. *Please let it be good news.*

"Where exactly? Okay, we'll head down there. Thanks for keeping me posted, Pauline."

After ending the call, he drove away from the park. "A bus driver reported seeing a child matching Zoey's description getting off at Disneyland. She told him she was meeting her parents, but then he heard the bulletin and called in. Park security's on the alert for her."

"This is good," Jane remarked. At least she hadn't been abducted.

Luke shot through a yellow light onto Harbor Boulevard. "I won't feel better till she's in my arms."

"I can imagine."

As Luke drove, Jane finally had a chance to consider this whole new side of him. While she'd imagined him continuing with his love-'em-and-leave-'em ways, he'd been transformed into a devoted father. The marriage couldn't have been easy on him, either. He deserved credit for standing by the mother of his child and trying to make it work. As for Pauline, Jane supposed she'd done the best she could, too.

Still, Zoey had deserved better than to be dragged from motel to motel. No wonder Luke harbored strong feelings about children's needs.

"I never really understood my wife," he commented as he veered around a double-parked truck. "During our marriage, I didn't have a clue how unhappy she was until she exploded at me. One day I thought everything was fine—or at least stable—and the next she stormed out. We hadn't even been arguing."

"Lots of people hold things inside," Jane observed. "My mom used to do that to avoid angering my dad."

"I suppose my mother did, too," Luke reflected. "She kept quiet for a long time, and then she blew, just like Pauline."

"What happened?" He hadn't talked much about his parents when they were in school.

"She left when I was four." He gripped the steering wheel. "Dad was a workaholic, plus she gave birth to three boys in a row, ending with me. I guess by the time I came along she felt trapped."

Jane couldn't imagine abandoning three young children. "Did she have joint custody?"

"No. In fact, we hardly ever saw her."

That *was* unusual. "Who raised you while your father was working?"

"A series of housekeepers," he said. "We acted up a lot. Eventually Dad cut back on his hours to be with us after school. He told me later he was afraid one of us might turn into a drug addict or an armed robber. Plus he mellowed a lot as he got older."

"Why didn't you see more of your mother?" Jane asked.

"Dad treated her departure as a betrayal. The mellowing part came later—much later. In those early days, whenever she visited or even phoned, he'd start a fight. After a while, she kind of gave up." Luke's shoulders slumped.

"That must have been hard on you."

"We saw her for birthdays and Christmas. That's about all." A light turned red, forcing the car to a halt. "She moved to San Francisco, plunged into art classes and started a new career."

"As an artist?"

Luke nodded. "I have to hand it to her. She did sur-prisingly well. She began teaching as well, to pay the rent." He accelerated as the light changed to green.

"What kind of work does she do?" Jane found the idea intriguing.

"I went to a gallery opening of her paintings a few years ago. Technically, they were well-done, but I found them bleak. Other people appeared to like them, though."

Talking about his mother provided a welcome diversion, so Jane dared to probe further. "What did you say to her?"

"That I was proud of her. It's the truth."

They were approaching the theme park when Luke's phone rang. He clicked a button and listened. "Yes… Where?"

From his responses, Jane gathered someone had spotted Zoey again. But Luke didn't look happy about it.

"What?" she asked after he finished the conversation.

"She tried to buy a ticket to Disneyland but didn't have enough money. When security approached, she ran off. They've got people fanned out around the area." His voice broke. "She must have panicked. I hate thinking of her so frightened."

"She made it all the way to Anaheim on her own," Jane pointed out. "She must be very resourceful."

In heavy traffic, they edged past the Magic Kingdom and California Adventure attractions. "Her school doesn't allow cell phones. If I had it to do over, I'd buy her one anyway."

Rather than dwelling on what might have been, Jane reviewed what she knew of the area. "Maybe she went to the Downtown Disney." There was no admission charge for the shopping and dining zone adjacent to the park, and the colorful store windows would appeal to a child.

"Good idea," Luke said. "Let's start walking. We can't see much from the car."

After parking, they hurried along a landscaped pedestrian avenue, pausing to show Zoey's picture to passersby and storekeepers. A few said they might have seen her but weren't sure, and none of them agreed on exactly when or where. New Orleans jazz rolling out of a restaurant created a festive air, but as the minutes turned into an hour and then longer, neither Jane nor Luke felt very optimistic. He called Pauline but she reported the police hadn't made any progress, either.

"She could be anywhere." Discouragement dulled Luke's tone.

"Let's assume she didn't act randomly." What other destination might have occurred to Zoey? Jane remembered the books at Hetty's house. "Eloise!"

"Excuse me?"

"She has two of those Kay Thompson books about Eloise, the girl who lives at a hotel."

"Zoey asked for them for Christmas," Luke explained.

"There are lots of hotels around here. Maybe one of them reminded her of the hotel in the book, the Plaza."

Luke regarded her with a spark of hope. "Maybe the Disneyland Hotel or... Wait! I took her to lunch a few months ago, right over there." He pointed toward a cluster of tall buildings bordering the Anaheim Convention Center a few blocks away. "She loves escalators and I'd noticed a really great one while I was attending a medical conference there. She and I rode up and down on it for half an hour."

"If she could find her way to Disneyland, I'll bet she could find that escalator again." Jane prayed that she was right.

They headed back to the car. Jane noticed the sky was growing dark. *Please, not another dead end.* She hated to think of his daughter lost and alone at night.

"No wonder Zoey identifies with Eloise. She's lived so much in motels," Luke said as they rounded a corner.

"You're a very perceptive father."

"Really? I'm always learning," he admitted. "Just when I think I've got a handle on her, I discover something new."

"I can tell you from my nanny days that not only are kids individuals, but they change right in front of your eyes." Jane had been astounded at how quickly her two small charges, an infant and a toddler, developed new skills and interests. And mischief-making abilities.

They zoomed through a yellow light, parked in the hotel garage and ran into the building. Jane stared around the grand lobby. Everywhere, guests strolled through gift and clothing shops, lined up at broad counters and, on the open mezzanine, buzzed around the restaurant and bar. How did you find one little person?

Luke stiffened. "There!"

On the huge escalator, a forlorn figure sat atop a step, riding downward. Blond hair wisped around a heart-shaped face and, even at this distance, Jane thought she perceived tear tracks on those cute cheeks. Her heart twisted for the drooping child.

"Zoey!" Luke's cry rang through the space.

The girl blinked. Her gaze swept the lobby and brightened as she fixed on the man at Jane's side.

Although Jane couldn't hear the small voice, there was no mistaking the word formed by her lips. *Daddy!*

Luke raced across the carpet and, as her step reached the bottom of the escalator, his daughter sprang into his arms. He caught her in midair and they whirled, laughing and crying, lost in each other.

At that moment, Jane felt a surge of pure joy for them both. And a tug of something beyond admiration for the loving man Luke had become.

Chapter Six

"I didn't mean to be gone so long." From the back of the car, a seat-belted Zoey spoke apologetically. "I 'spected you and Mommy to find me."

Luke didn't have the heart to scold her. Besides, what would be the point? Her gloomy expression on the escalator had shown how much she regretted running away.

He had spent a busy quarter of an hour notifying Pauline and the police that they'd found Zoey, and snuggling his daughter. She'd bubbled with stories about her adventure, admitting the security guards had frightened her but adding she was thrilled to have met costumed cartoon characters in the Disney shopping area. She'd also treated herself to a couple of ice cream cones along the way.

"Thank goodness you're safe." He'd barely introduced Jane so thought he should now explain who she was. "Jane's my new medical partner. I told you about her, remember? She walked all over Anaheim with me, hunting for you."

"I remember. She's your friend from school." To Jane, Zoey said, "Do your feet hurt?"

Luke chuckled at the question. Beside him, Jane managed to keep a straight face. "Yes. Thank you for asking. It's a good thing I already gave my dog his walk today, because I'm certainly not going to take him out when I get home."

"You have a dog?" Wistfulness underscored the question. "Is he like Weenie?"

"Who's Weenie?" Luke asked.

"That's Eloise's dog, Daddy," Zoey said. "He's a pug. What's a pug, exactly?"

"A lap dog." Not very precise terminology, he conceded, but the only small types he could picture were dachshunds and Chihuahuas.

Jane came to the rescue, as usual. "It's a Chinese breed with a cute wrinkled face. Stopgap is much larger. He's a spaniel mix."

"Can I meet him?"

"You bet. I live next door to your daddy."

Zoey fell silent. The rearview mirror showed traces of exhaustion on her small face. At least they'd found her. Thank goodness for Jane. Without her, Luke figured they'd still be looking.

She certainly had a gift for understanding a child's mind. If she really had a baby, he had no doubt she'd cope far better than most single parents. Including him and Pauline.

Not until they arrived at Hetty's house, its lights ablaze in the early darkness, did he remember about his ex-mother-in-law's heart condition. Much as he hated to drag Jane and Zoey into this, he couldn't allow the situation to continue.

First, however, he watched the blissful reunion as

Pauline and Hetty hugged Zoey and the little girl apologized to them both. Finally they trundled her off to bed, where she fell asleep almost before Luke finished pulling up the covers.

Hetty, although pale, asked the other adults to join her in the living room. "You might as well hear this together." Her voice quavered. "I'm sorry to say I can't take care of Zoey any longer. It's not because of what happened today. I'd already made the decision—in fact, that's what the argument was about."

Now he understood what had upset Zoey. Hearing her mom and grandma squabble over her future would upset any child.

Pauline shifted irritably on the couch. "Mom, there's only a month left on our tour. Zoey can't afford to skip that much school, and I can't just cancel without notice. I already missed tonight's performance—well, never mind about that. By the end of April, I'll be back. I'm sure you can handle her till then."

Luke noticed Jane studying Hetty with obvious unease. She apparently didn't consider the older woman in any shape to supervise a child, and neither did he.

The solution was obvious. "Zoey will stay with me. It's what I've wanted all along," Luke said.

"You're the one who made a fuss about putting her in school, and now you want to yank her out while she's still catching up with her lessons?" Pauline protested. "If you understood anything about parenting, Luke, you wouldn't even suggest it."

How unfair and unreasonable. Catching Jane's warning glance, however, Luke moderated his words. "You're right about one thing," he told Pauline. "Our daughter deserves stability. Transferring to a new school won't be a problem if she can stay there long-term. So I want to make this clear. She should live with me permanently, not just for the remainder of the school year."

"You? The doctor who's never there?" she scoffed.

"I'll be there," Luke said. "If necessary, I'll fight you in court. And this time, I won't give up."

WITH THIS DECLARATION, any last hint of Luke's old self-indulgent carelessness had vanished. To Jane, he resembled a deceptively lazy lion that had come roaring into his full power.

Still, she recognized the struggle evident on his ex-wife's face. What mother would choose to relinquish control of her child, even when circumstances made that the best choice?

"I have a house in a wonderful neighborhood, with lots of children around," Luke went on. "And I'm working fairly regular hours."

"How long will that last?" Pauline challenged.

"At least a year. I won't accept another position unless it will accommodate my responsibilities to Zoey."

"Being a parent isn't something you can master overnight."

"And you're such a great example?" He halted and regained control. "I realize I have a lot to learn, but I've been spending as much time as I can with her."

"I won't give her up!" Folding her arms, Pauline flounced back against the cushions.

Hetty released a long breath. "Luke, I think it's a lovely solution. Please promise you'll bring her to visit me often."

"Mom!" Pauline protested.

"Of course." Luke exchanged a warm glance with the elderly woman.

Pauline's eyes narrowed. "Zoey needs mothering. Okay, I've screwed up occasionally, but you have too high an opinion of yourself, Doc. You can't be all things to all people."

Jane wondered if she could help relieve Pauline's concerns. Gently, she said, "I live right next door, and I used to work as a nanny in college. That's not the same as being a mom, but I'll be there to help."

As soon as she finished speaking, she wondered what she'd just let herself in for. Despite her growing respect for Luke, or perhaps because of it, Jane needed to keep space between them. She could too easily fall in love with him, as she'd very nearly done in med school.

"Thanks, Jane." Emotion roughened his voice. "Pauline, please don't see this situation as negative. While we were married, you gave me the chance to pursue my career. Now it's your turn."

Her mouth twitched. "I suppose it *is* fair for you to take more responsibility," she conceded grudgingly. "But only until June. Once school ends for the summer, we'll have to see."

Luke sat braced as if for battle, but he simply nodded. "We'll revisit this issue then. I appreciate your flexibility, Pauline."

She eyed him skeptically. "I can come see her whenever it suits my schedule, right?"

"Certainly." He turned to the older woman. "Hetty, is it okay if I pick her up tomorrow morning around ten?"

The woman agreed, and Luke and Jane stood to leave. In the car, she asked, "Do you want me to come with you in the morning?" He might need a buffer, should his ex-wife suffer last-minute doubts.

And she *had* volunteered to help. For the little girl's sake, Jane meant to stay involved at least long enough to ease her move to Brea.

"I'd be grateful. I might even grovel at your feet," Luke teased.

"Don't do that. Stopgap will get jealous," Jane shot back. "So, what are your plans for fixing up Zoey's bedroom?"

"Er, right. Plans. Let's start with sheets on the bed— I saw a pink set in the linen closet." He navigated between the bright lights along Harbor. "I should get some groceries, too." Ruefully, he added, "I hadn't thought that far ahead. Thanks for prompting me, and for everything."

"Happy to help." The next few days ought to be interesting, Jane mused, and settled back for the rest of the ride.

ON SUNDAY MORNING, Luke awoke at six o'clock, his brain abuzz with projects for the coming week. Registering Zoey at school. Arranging a sitter for his on-call nights. Cooking and what else?

A few minutes later, he sat in the living room, staring at his list with the sense that he'd probably overlooked a lot. He hated to keep bothering Jane. If only he had family members to consult, but while his elder brother Quent had two kids, he and his wife lived almost four hundred miles away in San Francisco and always seemed absorbed in their own busy schedules.

Their middle brother, Kris, had already burned through two engagements and, as far as Luke knew, had zero experience with kids. Although he lived in L.A., he and Luke rarely spoke, partly because Kris often jetted around the globe putting together financial deals, and partly because, since childhood, the pair had always been competitive.

Setting the list aside, Luke got down to business, making Zoey's bed and assessing the contents of the pantry. On the Internet, he searched for "Food Kids Like" and stared dubiously at the results. Cheese, yogurt and eggs, okay, and certainly peanut butter, but what wild dreamer had added broccoli? He opted for a range of fruits and vegetables.

After showering and shaving, he drove to the supermarket and filled his cart with much more than he'd planned. He could hardly deprive his daughter of ice cream, and spaghetti sauce was on sale.

Passing the bakery section, he saw Minnie selecting pastries. She waved. "Is everything all right? You and Jane sure ran out of the potluck in a hurry."

"Family emergency." Luke filled her in.

"I can't wait to meet your daughter," the older woman responded. "Suzy Ching has a little sister about that age. She could help Zoey fit in at school."

"That's a great idea."

"I'll give them a call to let them know she's coming." Minnie set a package of Danish in her cart. "By the way, please don't tell Brittany you saw me buying this. It's for church. I'd have ordered something from her if I'd thought of it in time."

"They look delicious." Luke added a package to his growing pile. "Glad I bumped into you."

"Me, too. Good luck."

He headed for the checkout then hurried home. There was barely time to unload before he collected Jane and went to fetch his daughter.

Ready or not, a new phase of his life had begun.

AT HETTY'S HOUSE, Jane helped carry a couple of suitcases to the car while the excited girl loaded her father's arms with stuffed animals. According to her grandmother, Pauline had left already to rejoin the band.

"Take good care of my little angel," Hetty insisted.

"The best." Luke looked ready to skyrocket with happiness. "I'll give you a call to arrange a visit very soon."

"I'd love that."

"With all this stress, you should see your doctor about adjusting your medication."

"I'll call him tomorrow. That's a promise."

On the drive to Harmony Circle, Zoey peppered Luke and Jane with questions. How big was her bedroom? How close was the swimming pool? In her eagerness, she scarcely paused to hear the answers, and although Luke answered patiently, Jane sensed his restless energy humming through the air. Father and daughter were a matched pair in their high spirits.

When they halted in front of the cottage, Zoey let out a whoop. "We live here? It's like a fairy tale!" She stared at the porch. "Who are they?"

On the steps perched four girls, their hair colors shading from light brown to nearly black. Along with the trio of thirteen-year-old Little Foxes, Jane recognized Suzy's eight-year-old sister, Cindy. "It's a welcome party. Minnie works fast." Luke had mentioned their supermarket discussion.

"I don't see when she had a chance to contact anyone. She was on her way to church, and it's only eleven now," he protested.

"Minnie may be eighty-nine, but she can use a cell phone with the best of us." Plus, Jane thought in amusement, one should never underestimate the speed of the Harmony Circle grapevine.

Carly sprang up and began snapping pictures on her professional-quality camera. "You're going to be a star on our Web site," she told Zoey after introducing herself.

Her stepsister extended a plate of fresh-baked brownies. "I'm Brittany, and I made these for you."

"Wow." Eyes shining, Zoey selected a chocolate square. "Thanks."

"I'm Suzy and my sister Cindy's in third grade," said the black-haired girl. "She'll show you around school."

"If you forget your lunch money, I can lend you some," Cindy offered.

"Great!" The little girl spoke through a chewy mouthful.

Although Jane wished the girls had postponed their arrival until Zoey had a chance to unpack, their enthusiasm did a good job of melting the ice. Once Luke opened the door, they swarmed inside and set about arranging clothes and toys, chattering away at full volume. When Jane peered in, she saw Zoey standing on the bed directing the others like a miniature orchestra conductor.

She and Luke retreated. Judging by the giggles from the bedroom, nobody missed them.

"She's outgoing, isn't she?" Luke said as he arranged

children's books alongside his in the living room bookcase. "I was afraid moving around so much might have made her shy."

"I guess she learned to fit in." In a way, Jane envied the little girl's confidence. After relocating from Ohio, she'd felt lost her first month at medical school. She'd suggested forming a study group as much to make friends as to get help, although the academic support had been valuable.

Luke rocked back on his heels. "I hope she won't have problems adjusting to a new school. Her education's really been hit or miss so far."

Jane tried in vain to suppress a smile.

"What?" he demanded.

"I can't believe this is the guy who used to wander into study sessions in pajama bottoms with his hair falling in his face." She stretched her legs along the sofa, easing the soreness from yesterday's walking. "You've taken over my job. Now you're the one fussing like a mother hen."

"In my case, father hen," he corrected.

She feigned dismay. "Father hen? If you're this confused about gender, I'm canceling your surgeries."

His laughter echoed through the room. "Have you no respect for my brilliant skills?"

"I expected you to have more expertise with poultry, considering what a rooster you used to be," she returned.

He sobered at that comment. "Was I really?"

"Girls used to cry on my shoulder," she told him.

A crease formed between his eyebrows. "I hope you're kidding."

"Exaggerating, maybe." She couldn't resist adding, "You did tend to trade in girlfriends rather often."

"I was in no place careerwise to tie myself down. I thought they understood that." He'd apparently never imagined how much hurt he caused. "I figured once we stopped having fun together, my girlfriends would be happier if they found someone new."

"That's why you dumped them?"

"Yes. Why did you dump me?" he returned.

The question startled Jane. "Self-preservation," she blurted.

"You thought I'd treat you the way I treated everyone else?" he asked.

"Wouldn't you?"

Luke sank onto the floor and wrapped his arms around his knees. "No…well, maybe eventually. We had different goals, you'll recall. But I didn't see why we couldn't just have a good time while it lasted."

"For a man who's had a lot of relationships, you sure don't understand them," Jane observed.

"Remember, I grew up in an all-male household," he observed.

That raised an interesting question. "Why'd you become an ob-gyn? I mean, aside from saving lives, which is why we all became doctors."

It wasn't a high-paying specialty compared to radiology or plastic surgery, and obstetricians ran a higher risk of lawsuits than, say, dermatologists. In med school, Jane recalled him observing how much he enjoyed delivering babies, but that hardly seemed like the whole story.

Luke frowned. "I guess because I *wanted* to understand women."

"And do you?" she probed.

"After delivering more babies than I can count, and

counseling patients through pregnancies, menopause and serious illnesses…frankly, no," he said with disarming honesty.

"Well, that's straightforward," Jane conceded. "But don't you feel like you're doing them a disservice? They rely on you for guidance."

"I understand the medical issues," Luke clarified. "I've done everything in my power to learn how aging, illness and childbirth affect women's lives and what advice to offer. Focusing strictly on the patient makes it easy to be supportive, since my tastes and wishes don't figure into it. That's different from dating someone."

Jane conceded the point. "I have to admit, you've developed into an outstanding physician. Everyone raved about you at your former practice."

"You checked me out?"

"I have an obligation to my patients. Even if Sean *does* vouch for you."

"Of course. I'd have done the same thing." After dusting off his hands, he moved to the couch, so close that her bare feet grazed his thigh. Neither of them shifted away. "Why is it I feel more like myself with you than with anyone else? Your questions show me sides of my personality I've never taken the time to examine."

This was getting too personal, so she framed her answer carefully. "Maintaining a strong connection to the women I treat makes me really think about how I'm affecting them," Jane said. "Luke, high-power physicians and researchers do save lives, but often at the expense of understanding the impact they have on their patients as people."

"That's an interesting way of looking at it." He glanced toward the bedroom, where they could hear the cheerful sound of children's voices. "I think I'm going to learn more than I expected from working in a small practice."

"You've changed," Jane conceded.

"Overdue, I guess. Considering what an insensitive slug I seem to have been in the old days," Luke added on a lighter note.

"You certainly were."

"Ouch."

Jane searched for a bantering follow-up, but nothing came. She was too keenly aware of his strength coiled at her feet and of an almost physical ache to inhale his scent and run her hand across his chest.

As another burst of girlish chatter drew his attention toward the bedroom, he looked utterly contented and almost unbearably handsome. It struck Jane that she'd never found the right man because she'd always subconsciously compared everyone to Luke.

What a scary thought.

His head tilted toward her. "I feel like I've landed in a strange new world populated by charming female aliens. Thank goodness I have you as my translator and guide."

"Happy to oblige." Jane hoped he didn't notice how breathless she sounded, still off balance from her realization.

"You know what you are?" he went on.

"Tell me." *That you want all those things you weren't ready for, years ago. That you want them with me.*

"You're the sister I never had."

Sister? Well, of course. What an idiot she'd been, to expect Luke to turn into a card-carrying romantic. Disgusted with herself and peeved at him, Jane lurched to her feet, only to discover that they'd gone numb. "Darn it!"

He hopped up and caught her arm. "Are you all right? I thought you might fall over."

She extracted herself with a grimace. "Sore from traipsing around Anaheim yesterday," she covered. "I need to get going."

Disappointment clouded his gaze. "I hoped you'd stick around after our guests leave. You could bring your dog over. You did promise to introduce him to Zoey."

"Later. I'm having dinner with friends tonight and I've got to cook."

Luke quirked an eyebrow. "Would these friends be the Foxes?"

"The same." Her feet prickling from the returning blood flow, Jane worked her way toward the door. "I'll bring Stopgap to visit tomorrow. You can tell Zoey so she has something to look forward to if she starts feeling off-kilter."

He accompanied her to the hallway. "I'll do that."

"See you at work." Once the door clicked shut behind her, sheer nerves powered Jane home at a fast trot, and never mind how much her feet hurt.

What on earth had come over her, entertaining silly notions about her and Luke? He might have matured, but he was still a dangerous man to care about.

It was up to her and nobody else to make her dreams of family and children come true. The only question was—how?

She knew one thing for sure: whatever she decided, it wouldn't involve the maddening doctor next door.

Chapter Seven

Jane scarcely heard the conversation that evening around Alice Watson's dining room table. Usually she relished the lively discussions among the Foxes, but she couldn't focus on the debate over whether Alice and her boyfriend, George, should book a Mediterranean cruise or take a trip to China.

Was it the approach of her birthday, only a couple of weeks off, that had her feeling as if the world might end if she didn't come up with a dramatic plan for her future? Jane wondered. Perhaps she was overreacting to Luke's remark about regarding her as a sister. Yet if she didn't do something soon, she might dither along forever, childless and single.

She snapped to attention on hearing the word *adoption.* Tess Phipps, a divorce and family attorney, had just finished speaking.

"I'm sorry," Jane said. "I missed what you said. Are you adopting a child?"

"Not me. My clients." Tess fiddled with her bracelet. "I'm trying to transition from divorces to adoptions. I'm burned-out watching couples tear each other apart and destroy themselves financially. How anybody dares to get married is beyond me."

Newlyweds Brooke and Sherry raised a friendly storm of protest. Each claimed she was happier than she'd dreamed possible.

Tess dismissed their arguments. "Neither of you has been married more than a year. You're practically still on your honeymoons."

"Many of my clients save their marriages, with a lot of hard work," noted Cynthia Lieberman, a family counselor in her fifties.

The attorney's face scrunched. "A few people get lucky. But not everyone."

"Tess, where do your clients find children to adopt?" Jane asked. Around the table, faces turned toward her. Embarrassed, she realized her friends might think she was asking for personal reasons. "Just curious."

"Most work with agencies, including some that are overseas. Others set up Web sites and Facebook pages to promote themselves to pregnant women," Tess said. "There are adoption attorneys who run ads for babies, but I'm not sure I want to do that."

The talk shifted to other subjects and eventually to the street's newest residents, Luke and Zoey. The Foxes peppered Jane with questions about them, which she answered as briefly as possible. Discussing Luke felt like poking at a sore spot.

She was pleased when Maryam Hughes picked up the slack. "He and Zoey dropped by this afternoon to discuss day care. I'm going to watch her afternoons and on school holidays."

"They visited us, too," Sherry chimed in. "As his

landlords, Luke thought we had a right to know about Zoey moving in. As if we'd mind! In fact, I volunteered to let her sleep over the nights when he's on call."

"It's every Thursday, and occasionally on weekends," Jane said. "Isn't that inconvenient?"

"It'll be fun. The kids will enjoy having a new playmate."

Luke had certainly worked out his schedule fast, she mused. She ought to feel relieved that he wouldn't be depending on her for everything. Instead, disappointment squeezed her stomach.

Jane set down her fork, although she'd scarcely touched her lasagna or her garlic bread. Although she didn't *want* him to lean on her, it hurt to discover how easily she could be replaced.

For the first time since she'd joined the Foxes, she could scarcely wait for the evening to end. When at last she escaped, however, she found Brooke right on her heels.

"You forgot this." On the walkway in front of Alice's house, her friend held out Jane's bowl.

"Oh. Thanks." She noted with satisfaction that her friends had eaten almost all of her salad.

Brooke crossed the street beside her. "What's going on?"

"Sorry?"

"You're jumpy. Usually you're the calmest person I know."

Although tempted to skirt the topic, Jane opted for honesty. After all, Brooke *was* one of her best friends. Besides, Jane had never been good at playing her cards close to her chest. "Luke said he views me as a sister."

"So?" Brooke asked. "I thought you considered him a bit of a Romeo, anyway."

"It's just…insulting," Jane grumbled.

They halted in front of Brooke's house. "It could be worse. He could have compared you to his mother."

Jane had to chuckle. "I suppose that *would* be worse."

Never one to shrink from touchy subjects, her friend continued, "So you're thinking about adopting?"

Jane wished she hadn't opened her big mouth during dinner. "No."

"But—" Brooke prompted.

"Why do you assume there's a 'but'?"

"Because I know you."

Jane sighed. "I guess it's time to quit hoping Mr. Right will appear. I'll call the clinic tomorrow and make an appointment."

"Good. Your birthday's a week from next Friday, right? Unless you already have plans, I'm taking you out for dinner," Brooke said. "Hey! Wouldn't it be great if you're expecting by then?"

What a wildly optimistic timetable. Brooke, who'd become pregnant with Marlene by accident, had no idea how these treatments worked. "It'll be several weeks before I can even start trying," Jane explained. "I'd have to take a fertility medication to improve my chances of conceiving."

Brooke sighed. "Too bad." She perked up quickly. "About that birthday dinner. Is it okay if Renée comes, too?"

"Sure." The three of them would have a great time.

"Good. I'll invite her."

As they said good-night, Jane reflected how lucky

she was to have such a terrific friend. She could never stay down in the dumps for long around Brooke.

WITH JANE PERFORMING her scheduled surgeries on Wednesday morning, Luke barely got a chance to catch his breath at the office. In addition to seeing a full load of patients, he consulted with the physicians' assistant on a case and answered several lengthy phoned-in questions from patients. He rushed around so much that, in the hallway, he kept bumping into receptionist Edda Jonas, who had a gift for appearing where he least expected her.

He figured the mishaps must be his fault until his nurse, Pam, remarked in a dry tone, "You realize she's gaga in love with you."

"Edda?" he asked in amazement. "She can't be more than twenty-one."

"She's twenty-four," Pam corrected gently. "But never mind that. She treated Dr. Sawyer the same way when she was first hired, but she got over it."

"Let's hope so." Judging by Jane's remarks, Luke gathered he'd hurt some feelings at med school. That had been different, since it involved women he was dating, but he didn't intend to repeat that mistake even at a distance. "By the way, I wanted to ask you something. Is an hour a night too much homework for a second-grader?" Being the mother to three school-age youngsters made Pam an expert in his view.

"That depends," she said. "I assume that, coming from another school, Zoey has some catching up to do."

"Her reading's advanced, but in other areas she's behind." He could see how overwhelmed Pauline had been—or how careless—in home-schooling Zoey in first grade. Two moves during this school year hadn't helped, either.

"She'll pull it off." Pam winked. "She's got a smart father to help her."

"I'm trying." They'd spent a half hour last night just on Zoey's math assignment, which required her to measure the length of the kitchen by walking heel-to-toe. He'd tried it, too, and they'd burst out laughing at their wobbles, then had fun comparing the different sizes of their feet. That hadn't been so bad, he conceded.

As he swung around to replace the chart he'd been annotating, Luke narrowly avoided another collision with Edda. She beamed at him. "Oh, there you are!"

Pam made a choking sound, swallowing a laugh.

"Something I can help you with?" Luke asked as casually as he could.

"Tomorrow's hysterectomy patient had to reschedule because she's got bronchitis, and your C-section delivered last night. So you've got the morning free. Can we book patients?" Edda fixed her gaze on his face.

"Please run those matters by me, and I'll coordinate with Dr. Van Dam," Pam reproved. "Honestly, Edda."

"I was trying to save time!" the girl protested.

Pam narrowed her eyes. Taking the hint, the receptionist scooted away.

"You have to give her credit for caring about her work," Luke murmured.

"Word of caution," his nurse told him. "You might want to eat at your desk or go out. She brought in a huge fruit salad and a pile of sandwiches for the lunchroom. Baiting her trap, I suspect."

"That was generous of her." He found it hard to believe the receptionist had been thinking only of him.

"She asked me earlier whether a twenty-four-year-old was too young to be stepmother to a seven-year-old," Pam said pointedly.

Whoa—that *was* going overboard. "Thanks for the warning."

Retreating to his office, Luke munched the peanut-butter sandwich and carrot sticks he'd fixed, a twin to his daughter's lunch. Then, after shedding his jacket, he set to work organizing his books and hanging his framed medical certificates. He'd meant to do that last week, but his patients had taken priority.

From the hallway, he caught the familiar click of footsteps and a hint of Jane's springtime scent. Luke hurried out into the corridor. "How goes it?"

She turned, blinking as if pulled from a daydream. "I'm not here."

She looked real to him. "You're a hologram?"

"I mean, I just stopped by after surgery to pick up messages," she said.

Luke refused to let her escape that easily. She'd dropped by his house with Stopgap on Monday night, as promised, but almost immediately had to go out to check on a patient with pregnancy complications, and he'd seen far too little of her the rest of the week. "I could use a bit of advice."

She glanced at her watch. "Sure."

"You *do* get a lunch break," he reminded her.

"It isn't that. In fact, I cleared my schedule until three. I've got some personal stuff to take care of." Anxiety puckered her brow.

"Anything wrong?" He stood aside.

"No." Moving past him, she surveyed the office. "Looks better with your stuff on the walls."

From a cardboard box, he lifted a photo of Zoey, taken about two years ago. "Do you think this is too personal for my desk?"

"I think it's cute, if you can find space." She indicated the stacks of files and journals covering the flat surface. "Is that what you wanted my opinion about?"

"No. It concerns Zoey's behavior." He wasn't sure why but right now Jane was the one person he wanted to talk to.

"I wouldn't be surprised if she's going through a rough patch, with all the changes in her life."

"Actually, if anything, her behavior is too good. I'm afraid she's bottling up her emotions." He shoved a stack of magazines aside so he could sit on the corner of the desk. "She loves Maryam's house, adores her teacher and hugs me every chance she gets. This can't be normal."

"Sounds like the honeymoon period," Jane observed.

"Aren't those for married couples?"

"Cynthia Lieberman, our resident Harmony Circle psychologist, says they apply to anyone in a new relationship or situation."

Interesting concept. "So I can expect a period of adjustment ahead." He felt almost relieved to discover his intuition had been on target.

"Any contact with her mother or grandmother?" Jane asked. "That might help her release her feelings."

He'd kept his promise. "We went to see Hetty last night. She's doing much better without the stress of caring for a child." Luke had been relieved to see the woman's color improving and her energy level back to normal. "Zoey's talked to Pauline on the phone, but that isn't the same as seeing her."

Jane folded her arms. "She could benefit from therapy."

"True. She'd benefit even more from a sense of stability." He resented Pauline's insistence that they reevaluate where Zoey lived at the end of the school year. As far as he was concerned, returning her to a crazy life spent in motels shouldn't even be on the table. "I'm not looking forward to another legal battle with my ex."

In Jane's eyes, he caught a glimmer of moisture before she averted her face. Were those tears? "You look sad. What's wrong?"

She released a long breath. "I was thinking how lucky Zoey is to have such a loving father. Even when my dad was home, I always felt like I was getting between him and a ball game on TV."

"I'm sorry." Instinctively, Luke leaned forward to touch her shoulder. "Having a dad like that can affect the way a woman relates to other men in her life."

She jerked away. "I have no problem relating to the men in my life."

Her reaction startled him. "My apologies. I wasn't thinking."

Unreadable emotions flickered over her face. "It's all right. I have a lot on my mind."

Although they stood mere inches apart, he felt as if they were talking across a canyon. "Anything you want to chat about?"

"Afraid not." She stared out the window toward the parking lot. "Some things are too personal to share."

Luke had a sudden, intense longing to be the person Jane *did* confide in, the friend she trusted above all others. He'd done his best to convey that to her the other day, when he'd compared her to a sister. The problem was that sometimes his feelings for her strayed rather far from brotherly.

She turned toward him, mute appeal on her face. But for what?

Impulsively, Luke reached for her. For a moment, Jane stiffened, and then she fell against him and nestled into his chest.

In his arms, she felt feminine and so sweet that he longed to protect her. "Jane, whatever the problem is, let me help."

"You can't. But that's all right. I'm okay." With a trace of reluctance, she shifted back. "I might as well tell you, since you heard me discussing it with Brooke. I made an appointment at the fertility clinic."

The excitement of Zoey moving in had driven that conversation out of his mind. "You've decided to go through with it?"

"Not necessarily." She moistened her lips. "It's just a consult."

While Luke still believed two parents were better than one, he knew she had far better child-rearing skills than most single moms. "Whatever you decide to do, Jane, I'm on your team."

She relaxed a little. "That's good to know." Rising on tiptoe, she brushed a kiss across his cheek. It felt whispery and inviting. "You can be one hell of a man when you want to." Giving him a quick smile, she ducked out of the room.

The scent of her lingered after she'd gone. He wished she wouldn't keep fleeing. Whatever negative side of himself he'd presented to her back in medical school, he hoped that impression was beginning to change.

He wanted very much to keep her close. Even if, in order to do that, he had to leave more distance between them than he'd like.

Not until later, when he caught Edda staring at him in dismay, did it register that Jane had left a lipstick mark. As the receptionist stomped away down the hall, Pam handed him a tissue and grinned. "I'd say you took care of that problem."

"Exactly as I planned," he replied, and hoped she believed him.

But he hadn't planned any of this. Especially how he kept replaying Jane's kiss, and wishing he could be at her side for what might be the most important meeting of her life.

Chapter Eight

Several years ago, before Jane began referring patients to the fertility clinic, she'd visited it and met with the director. She'd admired the efficient operation, and found the curving walls and soft color scheme soothing.

Today, sitting in Dr. Linda Chandhuri's office, she couldn't have cared less about the decor. Her brain kept buzzing with what had just happened between her and Luke.

The moment his arms closed around her, she'd experienced a profound longing to melt into him. Having him hold her had felt like the most natural thing on earth, and the most alluring. Just like ten years ago.

Why feel this for a man who considered her a sister? But he *did* care. Ironically, his gentle concern, even though she knew it to be platonic, had touched a place deep in her heart.

She struggled to return her attention to the woman across the desk. Knowing Jane's medical expertise, Linda was skimming over the information about monitoring ovulation and taking a fertility drug to stimulate the release of mature eggs.

"Our latest figures show that our patients have about a twenty-five-percent chance of becoming pregnant each cycle," she said. "That's a couple of points above average."

"I'm aware of your excellent reputation." Several of Jane's patients had happily borne babies after coming here. "You have my complete confidence."

On her laptop, Linda clicked a few keys. "We update our donor information regularly. I'll show you in just a second."

"You have pictures?" Jane didn't expect that, although she'd be curious to see what the men looked like.

"No, but the descriptions are quite thorough. We recruit intelligent, healthy males from college campuses. As I'm sure you're aware, we screen each donor for his personal and family medical history. Here, have a look."

She swung the computer around to reveal a page of biographies. Reading through several, Jane noted that they included age, ethnic background, blood type, height, weight, scholastic achievements, sporting activities and other interests.

Scrolling down the document, she reflected that each donor appeared more ideal than the last. Yet she was choosing a father for her baby, not a contestant on a reality TV show. How could you tell the quality of the person? A shy janitor with a bad knee might make a superior parent to a bodybuilding Ph.D. candidate.

But whoever I choose won't be a parent. The donor, she reminded herself, would never hold the baby in his arms. Her child would never be cradled against its father's broad chest and feel the rumble as Daddy sang a lullaby.

Tears pricking her eyes, Jane turned the laptop back toward Linda. "I guess I'm not as ready for this as I thought."

"There's no hurry," the doctor assured her. "It isn't something you should rush into."

"I'm not. I've been putting it off for ages," Jane confessed. "If I don't have a baby soon, it may be too late."

"There are other ways to parent," Linda said sympathetically. "Adopting or taking in a foster child, for instance. Or simply being a devoted aunt."

"I'm an only child. Although I *am* a godmother."

"Many women feel pressured because their friends are having babies," the other woman murmured. "Counseling can help. Would you like a referral?"

"I have names already." Jane often recommended therapy to her patients. Yet she clung to the notion that she ought to be able to resolve this dilemma on her own. "Thanks for your time. I may be back sooner than you think."

"I'd love to help you realize your dreams."

As they shook hands, she noticed Linda's wedding ring. On the desk, a photo showed two beautiful, dark-haired children.

"I had fertility issues myself," said the other doctor, following her gaze. "Believe me, I understand how it feels to long for a baby."

The trouble, Jane mused as she walked to her car, was that her earlier encounter with Luke had left him stuck in her head. In each donor description, she'd instinctively searched for similarities.

She had to get over this fixation. Avoiding him obviously hadn't helped. Perhaps it was like having allergy treatments in which a patient, exposed to more and more of a substance, develops a tolerance for it.

It might be worth a try. Besides, she'd promised to help Zoey, and she didn't want to let the child down.

Even though a voice within warned that she was playing with fire, Jane decided she should see Luke again as soon as possible—like tonight.

LUKE HAD BEEN hoping Zoey would move past the honeymoon phase so they could iron out their problems and bond as a family. Too bad he'd forgotten the old saying that you should be careful what you wish for.

When he arrived at Maryam's house that evening, she showed him a small bruise on Zoey's arm and a similar one on another girl's leg. "They fought over a toy. I separated them as fast as I could, but I'm afraid they're a little worse for wear."

"Coretta pushed me," Zoey growled.

Luke crouched at her level. "She's younger and smaller than you."

She stared at him defiantly. "She pushes hard!"

"I've decided to keep them apart each afternoon until Zoey has a chance to unwind from school," Maryam told him. Behind her in the den, several children were playing a game of chutes and ladders. Zoey glared at the group as if their easy companionship came as a personal affront.

"That sounds like a good plan." When his daughter tugged at his hand, Luke said, "Get your backpack and we'll go."

"You get it," she commanded.

He raised an eyebrow. "Bossing Daddy around, are we?"

"I'm tired." She planted hands on hips.

To his annoyance, Luke realized that her stance reminded him strikingly of Pauline. He didn't want to come down hard on the child just because of that. Still, her attitude pushed the limits.

"Honey, you have to take responsibility for your possessions," he told her.

"What's that mean?"

Remember, she's seven years old, not seventeen. "It means carry your own stuff."

She studied him rebelliously until she saw that he meant it. Then, to his relief, she accepted defeat with good grace. "Okay, Daddy. I'm sorry." Off she went to fetch her pack.

"Kids do best when there are reasonable boundaries," Maryam said. "I wish all parents understood that as well as you do."

"My dad never tolerated nonsense. I guess I learned it from him."

Over dinner, Zoey chattered happily about her activities at school. Afterward, Luke washed the dishes while she stood atop a chair to dry them. "Dad, you missed a spot of salad dressing." She waved a fork.

"Where?" He peered at it.

"Right there." She held it closer, nearly poking him.

"Hey! I like my nose the shape it is."

She giggled. Luke took the fork and washed it again. There *was* a fleck of oil on the tines. "You have a good eye."

"Two good eyes," she corrected, and waved toward the window. "Yay! There's Stockup."

"Who?" Glancing out, Luke saw Jane and her dog marching up the walkway. His spirits lifted. He'd hoped she might stop by tonight, especially after she'd confided in him. "You mean Stopgap."

"I'll let them in." His daughter hopped down and raced for the door.

Luke had barely removed his apron before the dog leaped in and covered Zoey's face with slurps. She grinned with delight.

"Sorry if we're intruding." Jane straightened her figure-skimming blue sweater. "I took him out for a walk, and he made a beeline over here."

"If you wouldn't mind company, we could use some fresh air." Luke was hoping he and Jane might even be able to talk freely with Zoey's attention focused on the dog. "Do you think he'd behave if Zoey held the leash?"

"Please, please," his daughter begged Jane. "I'll make him be good, I promise."

"Let's give it a try." Jane handed the leash to the little girl, who gripped it with solemn intensity.

As they walked along Harmony Road in the mellow early-evening twilight, the scent of barbecuing drifted from across the street. A scattering of children swooped by on in-line skates, taking advantage of the recent arrival of daylight savings time.

Ahead of Luke and Jane, the dog adjusted his pace to Zoey's. "It's as if he takes into account that she's a child," he commented.

"Many animals have that instinct," Jane said. "Have you ever owned a pet?"

"Dad wasn't keen on letting animals in the house." Irwin Van Dam had been a stickler for order. In retrospect, Luke wondered how his father had fallen in love with their free-spirited mother. He supposed opposites really did attract—for a while.

"My father adored his Irish setter. If he could have taken Rusty with him on the road, he'd have done it. Mom was partial to cats." Jane broke stride as, ahead of them, Stopgap paused to sniff a freshly turned strip of dirt.

A sun-bronzed man in his thirties knelt on the lawn, removing a petunia plant from a six-pack. "Hello, Stopgap," he greeted the dog. "Don't eat my earthworms. They're good for the soil."

"He doesn't eat worms. He eats dog food." Zoey spoke with confidence, as if she personally fed the spaniel.

"As long as he doesn't chow down on my plants, I'm not complaining." The man nodded toward them. "Hi, Jane." To Luke, he said, "I'm Bart Ryan."

"Luke Van Dam, and this is my daughter, Zoey."

"I'd offer to shake hands but for some reason most folks aren't crazy about getting dirt all over themselves." The fellow grinned.

"Bart's a horticulturalist. A plant expert," Jane added for Zoey's benefit. "Those petunias are beautiful, but why aren't you waiting until Saturday?"

"Something special happening on Saturday?" Luke asked.

The gardener rocked back on his heels. "There's five big holidays in Brea. Christmas, Thanksgiving, New Year's, Fourth of July and Free Compost Day. This Saturday's Free Compost Day."

"What's that?" Zoey plopped onto the grass, the dog at her side.

"That's when we haul our empty containers down to the community center and fill them with compost," Bart told her. "It's a thank-you from the company that collects and recycles our lawn clippings all year."

"What's compost?"

"Old leaves and plants that break down into fresh soil," Jane explained. "It's great for our gardens. Bart's kind enough to let me put my trash cans in his truck so I can get them filled along with his."

"Want to come along?" Bart asked Luke. "I better warn you, hauling all that compost around is hard work."

"I've got muscles," Zoey informed him.

Bart's smile widened. "You're both welcome to join us. My truck seats four, and there's extra room for your containers in back."

That sounded like a fun outing for Zoey. "I don't need the compost, but I'd be glad to help," Luke said. "We'll be there."

"And by the way, the reason I'm not waiting till Saturday to plant these," Bart added as he lowered a petunia into place, "is that the soil in this bed's just fine already."

"It does look fantastic," Jane agreed.

When Stopgap butted his head against Zoey's leg, she climbed to her feet. "He's ready to go."

"Nice to meet you," Luke told the gardener.

"Same here. See you Saturday around eight."

As they strolled farther along the curving street, people waved, and a few came over to chat. A veteran of apartment dwelling, Luke had rarely known his neighbors before. Maybe one of these days he'd buy a house in a place like this.

By the time the foursome returned to the cottage, his daughter was yawning. "She gets herself ready for bed," he told Jane as Zoey headed for the bathroom. "In some ways, she's very grown-up. Raked me over the coals this evening for not washing the silverware carefully enough."

"I suspect she's had to be fairly self-sufficient," Jane ventured.

He decided the time was right to broach the topic that must be foremost on her mind. "How was your appointment at the clinic?"

"Well…"

A small figure emerged in the hall. "Read me a story, Daddy."

Not the greatest timing. Too bad Zoey hadn't dawdled in the bathroom the way she usually did.

"May Stopgap and I listen?" Jane asked.

"Sure." Zoey gave an excited hop. She chose *The Secret Garden*, and listened sleepily as Luke read the classic tale of an orphan girl. After a few pages, she dozed off, one hand resting atop Stopgap's head.

Luke and Jane tiptoed out. In the living room, he brought up the visit to the clinic again. "So, how did it go?"

She kicked off her shoes and sat on the couch. "It was weird."

"How?"

"It's hard to imagine carrying a child fathered by a stranger. You'd think I'd take a practical, scientific approach, but the reality of the whole thing hit me pretty hard."

He relaxed into an armchair. "Jane, does this have

anything to do with what I said at your house, about two parents being better than one?"

"Are you saying you don't believe that?" she countered.

"Well, in an ideal world, that *would* be best, but I didn't mean to put pressure on you."

She bristled. "Do you think I'm a wimp? Honestly, Luke, why would I put so much store in your opinions?"

That stung. "Because I'm your friend and I care what happens to you."

She poised as if ready to battle further, and then the fight went out of her. "I don't know why I'm so touchy tonight," she muttered.

"Tell me what happened." Obviously, *something* had got to her today.

"I guess I hadn't truly considered what it would mean if the father were anonymous." She fiddled with a long strand of hair. "I'd have no idea where my child got its laugh, or its dimples, or its talents. Half the baby's heritage would come from someone I've never met."

Luke chuckled.

"You think that's funny?" she challenged.

"No!" He lifted a hand apologetically. "It's just that earlier today, I got irritated with Zoey for defying me, and I realized that her attitude reminded me of her mother. Of course, I love everything about her, whether it comes from Pauline or me or just from herself, but a child's having half her heritage from an ex-spouse is a mixed blessing."

Jane's expression remained wistful. "Still, there's a part of me that believes a child should be conceived in passion."

Passion. Perhaps it was the word that made Luke

keenly aware of the rise and fall of her breasts and the curve of her mouth. Without thinking, he moved to sit beside her. "I should have gone with you."

"Why? So we could hold hands and pretend to be lovers?" She stopped, her cheeks coloring. "I don't know why I said that."

"Maybe this is why." Luke cupped her chin, relishing the velvety texture of her skin against his palm, and brushed his lips against hers.

For an instant, they seemed suspended in space, and then Jane kissed him back, a long, sweet taste. Wanting more, Luke angled toward her, but she slid back.

"Don't stop now." His words came out hoarse.

"We shouldn't do this," Jane replied. "I'd rather keep you as a friend."

"To hell with that. We're both adults. We can be friends *and* more." He traced his thumb across her cheekbone, and registered her sharp intake of breath. "Jane…"

She scrambled to her feet. "Someone ought to rip your clothes off, Luke Van Dam, but it isn't going to be me."

Disappointment arrowed through him. Breathing hard, Luke held himself tightly in place. Had he misjudged her response? No way in hell.

But he shouldn't have let his instincts run away with him, especially with Zoey in the next room. Nor did he have any right to ignore Jane's obvious reluctance.

"Still friends?" she asked.

"Of course." Now that she'd brought up the subject, he had a question of his own. "I've always regretted that we stopped being close in med school. I never understood why we couldn't go on hanging out together."

"Did it really bother you?"

"It hurt," he admitted.

"It did?" She seemed surprised. "Very much?"

He couldn't believe she was grilling him. "What kind of question is that?"

"I just wondered." Jane gave a low whistle and Stopgap padded into the room. She snapped the leash to the dog's collar. "I'm sorry if I hurt you, Luke. I never pictured you as the vulnerable type."

"I got over it," he said drily.

"See you tomorrow," she said.

"You bet."

After she left, Luke checked on Zoey and he found her curled beneath the covers, a sigh escaping her little mouth. Dreaming? A happy dream, he hoped.

In the living room, he turned on the news and was dozing off when the phone rang. Failing to recognize the number on the display, Luke answered cautiously. "Yes?"

"Dr. Van Dam?" demanded a brisk female voice.

"Yes."

"I'm Delilah Lincoln with Los Angeles County social services. I handle child welfare cases."

As far as he knew, the county had never been involved with his daughter, and Luke now lived in Orange County, not L.A. Warily, he said, "Working kind of late, aren't you?"

"Yes. This is an unusual situation," Ms. Lincoln replied wearily. "Are you acquainted with a young woman named Annie Raft?"

Obviously this call didn't concern Zoey. "I delivered her baby last fall, and we've stayed in touch. In fact, we spoke by phone about a week ago. I hope she's all right."

"I'm sorry to tell you she died in a motorcycle crash

last weekend. She was riding behind her boyfriend when a truck hit them."

His gut tightened. "I'm sorry. She was a wonderful young woman." He couldn't believe all that youth and promise had been wiped out. Annie had deserved better from life, and so had Brian. Then another thought occurred to him. "Who's taking care of her little girl?"

"That's the problem, Dr. Van Dam," the woman said. "The birth father relinquished all rights, so Annie's mother, Mrs. Brenda Raft, took the baby home with her. That seemed reasonable until this afternoon, when Annie's roommate came to see me. She'd found a handwritten will."

"Annie left a will?" Unusual for an eighteen-year-old. "Are you sure it's authentic?"

"I assure you, I do take my responsibilities seriously," the woman snapped.

He'd apparently hit a sore spot. "I didn't mean to imply otherwise."

"We compared the handwriting to other things she wrote, and it checked out," Ms. Lincoln continued more calmly. "In California, a handwritten will is legally valid."

"What does it say?" Annie must have had an important reason for drawing up such a document.

"She states that her mother abused her throughout her childhood, even though the matter was never reported to police. She calls Mrs. Raft unfit and insists that under no circumstances should she gain control of Tina."

That shook Luke. "I had no idea things were that bad. What will you do?"

"Until and unless a judge directs me otherwise, I will abide by the terms of the will," Ms. Lincoln said. "I will place six-month-old Tina Raft with the guardian her mother named."

Still trying to absorb the shock of Annie's death, Luke asked distractedly, "And who would that be?"

"That would be you, Dr. Van Dam," said Ms. Lincoln.

Chapter Nine

The medical profession demanded flexibility, Jane had learned. Patients canceled appointments, or rescheduled them so they had to be worked into an already packed day. And while general practices could refer overflow patients to a walk-in clinic for routine illnesses, pregnant women had to be seen by an obstetrician.

Such was the case with Olivia Riley, a forty-year-old executive in her sixth month. Although she was Luke's patient, he'd canceled his Thursday-morning appointments—only two, and both arranged on short notice— citing a personal emergency. Jane tried to put the possibilities out of her mind and focused instead on Olivia's chart.

"As the nurse explained when she called with your test results, your blood sugar levels are higher than we'd like," Jane told the woman seated in her office, which she'd chosen over an examining room for this discussion. "They put you on the borderline of gestational diabetes. While there's no immediate danger, we'd like to lower those levels."

Olivia, a tall brunette in an elegant maternity dress,

clutched the hand of her husband, Fred, who scowled. "I don't understand how this could happen. My wife takes excellent care of herself."

"There's nothing she could have done to prevent this," Jane assured them. "Both genetics and age may be factors. The good news is that gestational diabetes can be managed."

Olivia studied her uncertainly. "Will this harm the baby?"

"Not necessarily." Jane outlined the course of treatment, starting with a customized meal plan drawn up by a dietician. "Let's see if a special diet plus exercise will bring your blood sugars under control."

"And if not?" grumbled Fred. "What are you going to do then, Doctor?"

Obviously, his wife's condition aroused a strong protective instinct, Jane reflected. She admired him for that. "Then we'll begin insulin therapy. That should bring those glucose levels down fast."

As she answered their questions, the pair swayed toward each other, drawing strength from their partnership. Gradually, their tensions eased as they accepted that, despite this new issue, their baby was fine.

As they were leaving, Fred Riley shook Jane's hand. "Whatever I can do, just say the word. I'm here for my wife."

"Encourage her to eat right and exercise," Jane told him. "Other than that, your love is the most important thing."

As she watched them go, it hit her that, if she got pregnant and developed a complication, she'd have no husband to watch over her. Even in a normal pregnancy, she'd miss that sense of shared commitment.

Maybe she should take Linda's advice and become a foster or adoptive mom. But that wasn't an easy option, either.

From the hall, an infant's babbling caught her attention. One of the delights of working in this office was seeing the babies who sometimes accompanied their mothers to postpartum checkups.

Hurrying out, Jane spotted Luke surrounded by a knot of women. In his arms wriggled a small girl about five or six months old, a pink bow bobbing in her blond hair as she waved a stuffed bear.

"Ba-ba-ba!" she announced proudly, and smacked him in the face with it.

"Whose little charmer is this?" Jane asked.

"Mine." Luke gave her a guarded smile. "Jane, I'd like you to meet Tina Raft. Soon to become Tina Van Dam."

Surely he hadn't forgotten to mention *another* daughter. But where…?

"She just fell into his lap!" cried Edda, tracing the baby's cheek with her finger. "Her mom died and left her to Dr. Van Dam in her will. I mean, it's sad and everything, but isn't that cool?"

"Well," Jane said, and discovered she'd run completely out of words.

LUKE COULDN'T SHAKE the smell of unwashed sheets and spoiled food from Mrs. Raft's apartment. Plus, although Annie's mother had insisted she lived alone, a dirty man-size sneaker had protruded from beneath the couch.

"You can't just hand my granddaughter to this man!" Brenda had raged at the social worker.

Delilah Lincoln, a no-nonsense, clipboard-toting

Send For
2 FREE BOOKS
Today!

I accept your offer!

Please send me two free *Harlequin American Romance*® novels and two mystery gifts (gifts worth about $10). I understand that these books are completely free—even the shipping and handling will be paid—and I am under no obligation to purchase anything, ever, as explained on the back of this card.

354 HDL EYU2   **154 HDL EYPR**

Please Print

FIRST NAME

LAST NAME

ADDRESS

APT.#   CITY

STATE/PROV.   ZIP/POSTAL CODE

Visit us online at
www.ReaderService.com

Offer limited to one per household and not valid to current subscribers of *Harlequin American Romance*® books.

Your Privacy — Harlequin Books is committed to protecting your privacy. Our Privacy Policy is available online at www.eHarlequin.com or upon request from the Harlequin Reader Service. From time to time we make our list of customers available to reputable third parties who may have a product or service of interest to you. If you would prefer for us not to share your name and address, please check here ☐.

▼ Detach card and mail today. No stamp needed ▼

H-AR-09/09

black woman who'd met him in front of the building, hadn't retreated. "You are entitled to hire an attorney," she'd responded. "In the meantime, we're abiding by your daughter's will."

Luke had crossed the cluttered living room to the crib. Since he last saw Tina, she'd gained a healthy amount of weight and learned to sit unaided. "You're growing up fast," he'd said. "Remember me?"

"Ba-ba." She'd shot him a winning smile.

"Do you know anything about children?" Brenda had challenged. "My daughter probably had a crush on you. What're you, some playboy?"

"I was her doctor, not her boyfriend, and I have a seven-year-old daughter who lives with me. I share custody with my ex-wife," Luke had responded while registering Tina's striking resemblance to Annie.

"You're willing to raise Tina as your own?" Ms. Lincoln had asked.

"Absolutely." He knew it wouldn't be easy adding another child to his household, but he'd promised Annie she could count on him. She'd trusted him with her precious daughter, and he intended to honor that trust.

"This isn't fair. You're pushing me aside because he's a big shot," Brenda had snarled.

"Your daughter felt very strongly about this," the social worker had replied. To Luke, she'd added, "You can take her with you today. We'll conduct the home study shortly." She'd explained earlier that her department would need to do a formal interview, a background check, a financial review and an inspection of his residence.

Now here he stood, his car stuffed with child-care equipment and the baby curling against his shoulder.

He'd phoned Maryam, who'd agreed to start watching Tina this afternoon. Zoey had been delighted by the news that she was going to have a sister, and could hardly wait to show her off to the Little Foxes.

A pucker formed between Jane's eyebrows. "How exactly did this miracle occur?"

He sketched his friendship with Annie, her sudden death and her allegations about her mother. "She relied on me to protect her child. So here we are, getting better acquainted."

"The poor little thing." Jane touched the baby's curly hair. "You seriously intend to keep her?"

"I do." He refused to worry about the challenges ahead. "I know raising two daughters will be harder than raising one, but…"

"About four times harder," remarked Pam.

"I appreciate the warning." With proper organization and prioritizing, and a lot of love, he'd manage. Plenty of other parents did. "Can we talk in my office?" he asked Jane.

"Sure. Mind if I hold the baby?"

"Please do." He handed over the squirming infant.

As they walked, a small hand tightened on a strand of Jane's brown hair. Barely flinching despite what appeared to be a hard tug, she cooed to the little one soothingly.

"You're a natural," Luke said.

Jane gave him a rather sad smile. Was she still troubled about her visit to the clinic? Before he could ask, she said, "By the way, I suggest you phone Tess Phipps."

"I'm sorry—who?"

"She's an attorney who lives on our street and handles

adoptions." She provided the firm's name. "She'll be especially helpful if the grandmother sues for custody."

"That's a great idea." He hadn't had time to think that far ahead.

As they stood in his office, Tina yawned, ready for a nap. He had to get her settled and see to a swarm of other details, but first he wanted advice on a matter that had been bugging him as he tried to come to terms with Annie's death.

"As I mentioned, I met Tina's mom at a maternity clinic for teens in L.A.," he told Jane. "She deserves a memorial, not just a bunch of flowers at the accident scene but something that will live on. Do you think Brea could use a similar clinic?"

Jane adjusted her grip on Tina. "Luke, it's a wonderful idea. Sometimes you put me to shame."

"Why on earth would you say that?"

"I'm the one who's determined to help women one-on-one, and I do volunteer occasionally, but it never occurred to me to consider doing something like that."

"So you think there's a need?" he persisted.

"Orange County may be affluent, but there are pockets of poverty everywhere." Idly, Jane rubbed her cheek across the little girl's head. "There are several unused suites at the hospital. I'll speak to Wendy Clark. She took over as hospital administrator a couple of years ago and she's made a lot of improvements, like the new birthing center. She's very forward thinking."

"I'll take care of it," Luke assured her. "I didn't mean to impose on you. Although I'd be thrilled to have you participate."

"Believe me, I'll let you know if you're imposing,"

Jane answered. "As for Wendy, let me make the initial contact. If she's interested, we'll set up a meeting."

"Thanks," he told her, "more than I can say." In the quiet moment that followed, he heard a truck rumble along Central Avenue. "About last night. I hope you aren't upset."

"I'm not going to run screaming into the woods just because you kissed me," Jane said tartly.

"Good," he told her, "because if you did, I'd have to chase you down and use all my powers of persuasion to bring you back."

"Is that a threat or a promise?"

"A promise. And I'm very persuasive." So was she, Luke conceded silently. "Being around a baby brings a glow to your face. Did you know that?" Without thinking, he reached toward her...and received a fidgeting Tina in response.

"And holding an infant makes a man irresistible," she replied. "To any female from nineteen to ninety."

"I'm counting on that," Luke admitted. "This is going to be a big adjustment for everyone."

"Guess you could use someone with nanny experience. I'll stop by tonight." She chuckled as the baby chewed on his lapel. "Might want to buy a pacifier, too."

"Or a teething ring," Luke said. "Well, we're off to the sitter."

"Good luck."

"I have a feeling I'm going to need it."

He set off, a little intimidated by the prospect of accommodating the afternoon's full slate of patients and surviving an evening crammed with adjustments involving the girls. Somewhere along the line, he hoped he'd find the right rhythm to make everything work.

He'd better do it fast. Because he had a notion the daddy two-step had just been transformed into a dance marathon.

DURING THE NEXT FEW DAYS, Jane spent most of her spare moments helping with Tina and Zoey. Luke might already be a dad, but he had a lot to learn about changing diapers, managing meals and calming temper tantrums.

The whole neighborhood pitched in. Sherry agreed to watch both girls during Luke's on-call nights. Brooke volunteered to handle his basic baby-supply shopping when she stocked up for Marlene, while Minnie began crocheting a crib blanket.

Jane hoped nobody suspected how often, on arriving home from work, she stomped through the house and complained to her dog. She adored the girls, but how frustrating! While she yearned for a baby, all around her the little creatures turned up like dolls under everyone else's Christmas trees. Brooke had gotten pregnant by accident, Sherry had become a stepmother to twins, and now, out of the blue, a social worker handed Luke this sweetheart.

If only babies truly did grow in cabbage patches, Jane might have a chance, she mused the following Saturday as she and Bart rolled homeward with a load of compost-filled trash cans bumping in the bed of his pickup. Luke had run into some last-minute issues getting the kids ready and had promised to meet them at Jane's house for the unloading.

"Got your garden all planned?" Bart asked as they bounced down Central Avenue. His truck drove like a tank.

"Yes. I'm going to rotate the tomatoes, as you recommended." Jane liked taking a scientific approach to gardening. "And I'll buy disease-resistant varieties."

He slowed as cyclists flocked past on racing bikes. "Throw in a few heirloom varieties for the taste."

"But they're so vulnerable to wilt."

"What's life without taking chances?" The shaggy gardener turned into Harmony Circle. "This year I'm planting a whole section of red corn. Maybe I'll regret it, but I love the stuff."

"That's you. A real adventurer."

"As long as I'm in my own backyard." Bart laughed. He was such a nice fellow, Jane thought. Too bad he didn't make her heart beat faster.

They halted in front of her house. Her gaze flew to Luke, who was waiting and looked ready for action in close-fitting jeans and a black T-shirt that emphasized his broad shoulders.

Beside him, Zoey sat on the grass playing with Tina. With their hair similar shades of blond, the girls seemed like sisters already.

They were joined by Carly Lorenz, who swung her camera toward the truck. Taking shots for the community scrapbook, no doubt.

"That must be the baby I've been hearing about," Bart commented, cutting the engine. "Sure is cute."

"I didn't think you cared for children." Jane hopped down from the cab, waved at the others and circled behind the truck while Bart lowered the tailgate. "I remember you saying once that you pre-ferred plants."

"I used to think that." He jumped into the bed and unhooked a stretch cord from around the cans. "Then I met Brooke's little doll. Never realized kids were so fascinating."

Luke joined them in trundling cans to the rear yard, where they dumped the rich black compost onto Jane's garden. Carly recorded every move and Zoey provided a running commentary for Tina's benefit.

Afterward, Luke accompanied Bart to unload the gardener's share of their haul. Left with the youngsters, Jane raked compost into a thin layer across the plot.

"My grandma used to grow tomatoes." Sitting on a blanket beside Tina, Zoey rested her chin on uptilted knees.

"Would you like to help me plant next weekend?" Jane asked.

"Okay."

She detected a lack of enthusiasm. "You don't have to."

"I want to," Zoey protested. "Honest."

"Is something bothering you?"

Carly knelt for a close-up of Tina, who was chewing on a teething toy. "They're sad because they miss their moms."

That showed a lot of sensitivity for a thirteen-year-old, Jane reflected. "I'm sure they do."

"My mother called yesterday," Zoey piped up. "She and the band are going to Vegas. Where's that?"

"About a five-hour drive from here. Or more, depending on traffic." Since moving to Southern California, Jane had learned to calculate distances in driving time.

"Maybe she'll come visit." The longing in Zoey's voice tugged at Jane's heart.

"I only see my mom about twice a year since she moved to New York," Carly said.

Zoey gave her a puzzled look. "Your mom lives here."

"Diane's my stepmother. My real mom's kind of flaky. Maybe I shouldn't say so, but it's true." She lowered the camera, and explained that she used to live with her father, Josh Lorenz. Then he'd fallen in love with their neighbor, Diane, and they'd married a little over a year ago. Now the newly formed family of four shared Number 12, Harmony Road. "Brittany and I are stepsisters, like you and Tina."

"I like having a sister," Zoey said, although to Jane her enthusiasm sounded a bit forced.

"I've got a brother, too. He's nine months old." Carly angled to shoot Jane, who was prying out weeds. "His name's Wesley and he lives in New York. I hardly ever get to see him."

The girl's openness impressed Jane. She hoped it would help Zoey accept her own situation.

From inside the house, where she'd banished the dog to keep him from digging in the loose soil, arose a volley of barking. "That's *my* brother," Zoey announced. "Isn't he, Jane?"

"He certainly thinks so."

Carly tucked her camera into its case. "Zoey, do you and Tina want to come back to my house? Brittany's baking sweet rolls and I'm sure she'll have plenty for us." To Jane, she offered, "I'll look after the baby, and I'll walk them home when they're ready."

"How kind of you. You'll have to ask their father, though."

They didn't have long to wait before Luke rejoined them, his T-shirt clinging to his torso and a sheen of sweat on his forehead. When Jane explained what Carly had suggested, he agreed and thanked the girl. "You have to keep an eye on Tina every minute," he cautioned.

"I know. I babysit a lot." After retrieving the stroller, the teenager demonstrated her skills by tucking the baby inside and strapping her expertly into place.

"You girls have fun," Jane told them.

Zoey gave her dad a hug, and then gave Jane one, too, and off they went.

"She's certainly taken to you. My daughter has good taste." Luke stretched, a move that outlined his muscles with imposing definition. "Plus, you seem to have a green thumb. Bart sang your praises."

"Really? He's usually not much for conversation."

Luke claimed the rake from where she'd leaned it against the fence and set to work breaking up clods of compost. "That's funny. He hardly stopped talking about you."

"What on earth did he say? Aside from the part about my thumb, I mean." Jane rubbed her shoulder where the muscles ached from all the lifting.

"'Some say Renée's the prettiest lady in the neighborhood, but they're wrong. It's Jane,'" Luke quoted as he chopped a lump to smithereens.

"Bart said that?" she asked, astonished.

Luke whacked the soil again, harder than seemed necessary. "He likes your hair longer."

"He noticed my hair?"

"What's going on between you two?" Leaving off raking, Luke turned toward her. "Not that it's any of my business."

The absurd notion crossed her mind that he might be jealous. *Oh, right.* "Nothing."

Retrieving the hose, he washed off the rake's tines. "Well, whenever you'd like some heavy lifting, don't hesitate to give me a call. Bart's not the only guy in the neighborhood who can work the soil."

"You have your hands pretty full already."

"I have to admit, that's true." He turned the hose on his dirt-covered knees, sending up a fine spray that plastered his jeans and T-shirt against his taut frame. "Yesterday when I brought the kids home from day care, the Little Foxes were waiting on my porch with another baby. I thought seriously about hanging a U-turn and heading for the border."

"Was it Marlene?" Jane guessed.

"Minnie's granddaughter." He studied her from beneath a sweep of damp hair. "I have a favor to ask."

"Shoot."

He switched off the water and began coiling the hose. "Would you check my porch in the mornings? If you see a basket that's squirming, would you please just take it and not tell me?"

She burst out laughing. "Well, thank goodness."

"Thank goodness what?"

"Thank goodness the hapless med student is still alive somewhere inside that take-charge man of the world."

"I have far more hapless-med-student moments than I'd like to admit," Luke conceded.

Jane wished she weren't so acutely aware of how appealing he looked, hot and wet, or of the intensity with which he watched her. Memories flooded back, of his mouth on hers and his hand reaching to draw her to him.

"Since the kids are gone, we could fix lunch together," he said. "How about another cooking lesson? After I clean up, of course."

She fought the image of him stripping for the shower.

And of her slipping beneath the spray beside him, letting the water sheet off their skin as they moved against each other…

Too dangerous. She was *not* ready for that.

Luke had matured a lot, and his proposal to establish a maternity clinic for teenagers showed how involved he was becoming with the community. The suggestion had met with enthusiasm from the administrator, who'd agreed to meet with them both next week. But getting close to him still didn't seem like a wise idea. He'd been here less than a month. What was the rush?

From indoors, Stopgap's barking provided a welcome distraction. "I've been neglecting my faithful companion," Jane said. "Another time, okay?"

Luke ducked his head. "You're right. I've got laundry and dishes piled up." He looped the last bit of hose into place. "I'm sorry about next weekend."

She had no idea what he meant. "What about next weekend?"

"Somebody mentioned that Friday's your birthday. I'd like to take you out, but I drew on-call duty that night."

"That's okay. I have plans," she told him.

"Well, good." He looked far from pleased, though. "They don't happen to involve— Never mind. Have a great time. And by the way, I like your hair longer, too." With a wave, he strode off.

Jane carried the rake to the garage. Luke *was* jealous. The discovery left her feeling deliciously desirable.

But also grimy and disheveled. And her hair was a mess. With a start, she realized she'd forgotten all about Renée's makeover offer. She hoped her friend still had an appointment available.

Perhaps it was just as well that she wasn't having lunch with Luke. But she couldn't help wishing, just a little, that she could see the expression on his face when he glimpsed the new, improved Jane.

Well, the effect should last for more than a day. So perhaps she'd get that pleasure, after all.

Feeling energized, Jane whistled her way into the house.

Chapter Ten

"I can't go to bed." Zoey planted her feet firmly in the middle of the living room on Monday evening. "Mommy might come visit."

"What?" After a peaceful weekend, Luke's daughter had nearly melted down over a missing hairclip this morning. According to Maryam, she'd been unusually cranky after school as well, and she'd hardly touched her supper. "Did she tell you that on the phone yesterday?" Pauline usually called on Sundays, and occasionally during the week.

"No." The little girl played with a bit of ribbon on her nightgown. "She said she's in Vegas."

"I know." His ex-wife had enthused about the band's gig at a well-known lounge. "If she decides to drive out, it probably won't be until they're finished."

"They don't play on Mondays," his daughter responded. "Jane says it's a five-hour drive. So she *could* come."

That explained Zoey's restlessness. She assumed her mom would gladly drive that far to see her daughter on a free day. Luke certainly would have.

"If she planned to come, she'd tell us," he informed Zoey.

"Not if it's a surprise."

From his bedroom, where he'd put Tina's crib, he heard the baby fussing. "Honey, it's your bedtime, and I've got to feed the baby. I promise I'll wake you if your mother arrives."

Zoey switched to another complaint. "We haven't had a bedtime story for ages. You're always too busy with Tina."

The grumbling in the bedroom rose to a wail. "I'll tell you what," he said. "Give me half an hour to take care of Tina. Then I'll read to you."

"Just you and me? Without her?" Zoey asked petulantly.

"I'll put her back to bed," he promised. Zoey had a right to private time with her father.

"Well, okay." Out she plodded, dragging her feet.

He kept his promise. A short while later, they cuddled up on the couch with *The Gardener* by Sarah Stewart, about a little girl planting a garden during the Depression. Zoey had picked it out at the bookstore the previous day.

Curled in his lap, Zoey asked, "Let's plant our own garden."

He'd like to do that, but he couldn't dig up the yard of a rental. "The house belongs to Sherry. How about if we plant vegetables in pots?" Luke proposed.

That seemed to satisfy her. "What kind of vegetables?"

"The small kind." He supposed he could ask Bart for advice. On the other hand, Luke had mixed feelings about the fellow. All those compliments about Jane…

and why had she looked so pleased? "Radishes are small. I think there's a patio type of tomato. What else would you like?"

"How about pumpkins?"

"They're kind of big."

"Not miniature pumpkins!"

He sighed. "I'm guessing the plants are still large, but we'll find out. Now it's time for you to go to sleep."

"All right." She burrowed into him, arms tightening around his neck, and planted a smooch on his cheek. "Night, Daddy."

"Night, sweetheart." He scooped her up and launched himself to his feet. "Oops! What's that lead weight in my arms?"

She giggled. "It's me."

"Me, who? I don't see anybody." As they headed toward her bedroom, he pretended to stare all around, playing a game they'd enjoyed when she was younger.

"I'm here." Zoey stuck her face in front of his.

"Where'd you come from?" he asked in feigned astonishment.

"You're silly. Whoa!" She shrieked happily as he pretended to drop her on the bed, then swooped her to within a few inches before letting go.

He should be soothing her to sleep, not getting her excited, Luke reflected, but Zoey deserved a little fun. "Guess I goofed."

She reached for another hug. "I love you, Daddy."

"And I love you, angel."

"Don't forget to buy pots," she said.

"I'll put 'em on my list."

That list, Luke reflected as he switched off the light,

never seemed to get shorter, no matter how many things he bought. But he didn't mind.

In the living room, he checked his e-mail. As usual these days, scanning the messages saddened him, because of the reminder that there'd never be another of Annie's cheerful communications. How fragile life was, and what a sacred trust she'd left him.

Tomorrow, he and Jane planned to meet with the hospital administrator. Finding a suitable suite of rooms for the memorial clinic was the first step. They'd require financing and other physicians to donate their time, but he hoped that, by the time Sean returned, it would be well enough established to thrive without Luke.

He felt a twinge of concern. Perhaps he could stick around Brea longer than he'd initially intended, to make sure the place found firm footing and to see Zoey through to the end of the next school year. But knowing his cousin's dedication to working with the underprivileged, Luke knew Sean would do a terrific job with the clinic, too.

Returning his attention to his in-box, he found notes from both his parents, whom he'd informed about Zoey coming to stay with him and about Tina's arrival. His father wrote that he planned to make the three-hour drive from Santa Barbara to visit them next month.

As for Luke's mother, she didn't mention the children or her other two grandkids, even though his brother Quent's family lived near her. Instead, she wrote about her latest art exhibit, attaching images of two rather stark paintings.

Luke recalled Zoey's hope of seeing Pauline tonight. How often as a child had he fantasized about his mother returning? For both women, marriage and children had proved too heavy a burden. Or simply too much trouble.

With his replies, he attached a picture he'd shot on Sunday of the two girls playing together. Luke also summoned a couple of words of praise—"original" and "striking"—for his mother's paintings. They were original, striking and ugly, but he refrained from saying that.

Then he sprawled on the couch and tuned the TV to an L.A. Lakers game. Since he'd be on duty this weekend, he'd better relax while he could.

LUKE HAD LIKED Wendy Clark the first time they met, when Sean introduced them, and he liked her even better on Tuesday. The forty-something administrator of the North Orange County Medical Center sparkled with enthusiasm as she showed him and Jane a suite formerly occupied by a drug rehab program that had moved to larger quarters.

"I've been hoping to find a use for it that would serve the community," Wendy said. "Your idea hit the mark."

He gazed appreciatively at the soft green walls. There wasn't much here, just basics like a built-in front desk, examining rooms and a lab space for collecting specimens, but compared to the clinic in L.A., it seemed luxurious.

"A lot of small medical centers have failed in Orange County in the past few decades, losing ground to the megahospitals. I'm not going to let that happen here," Wendy said. "I want to expand our mission and make us stand out."

"The *Orange County Register* runs a lot of human-interest stories." Luke had noticed how reader-friendly the newspaper was. "I'll bet they'll jump right on this."

"Is there any furniture or equipment left over from the old birthing facilities that we could use?" Jane put in. "That might give us a start."

"Great idea." Wendy made a note. "We stored some things in a warehouse until we could figure out where to donate them. Now we can use them ourselves. I love it!"

The three of them continued discussing the issues: how the hospital community-relations department might network with doctors' groups to secure volunteers. How a staff grant writer could apply for government funding. How they might use publicity to inspire local donors.

"I'll talk to service groups," Wendy agreed. "Put on your thinking caps these next few weeks, and among us maybe we'll come up with the names of some angels."

"Will do," Luke assured her.

When Wendy's cell rang, she excused herself to deal with a staffing issue. Gazing around, Luke felt a lump form in his throat. "Annie would love this."

"I wish I'd met her," Jane said thoughtfully.

"I just hope her confidence in me wasn't misplaced," Luke admitted.

"What do you mean?"

Last night, when he'd finally had a few spare moments to think, he'd begun considering the long term. "She assumed I'd be able to raise Tina by myself, but as I told you, I've always believed two parents are best."

"I didn't have two parents, not in the true emotional sense," Jane pointed out. "Neither did you. We turned out fine."

"Did we?" he asked.

"You don't think so?" She studied him challengingly.

"I'm divorced. You're considering having a child alone. Maybe if we'd had a better parenting model…"

"Spoken like an academic!" Jane returned.

"Okay, better moms and dads."

"Then what?" She leaned against the front counter. "We'd have married Mr. and Ms. Wonderful and each produced two-point-five children with perfect teeth?"

He laughed. "Or simply found happiness."

"Why do you assume this isn't happiness?"

Just as in med school, she had a way of turning a subject around and forcing him to examine it from a fresh angle.

"We have it pretty good," she continued.

"Half the time I'm running on empty," Luke countered.

"There's a line from a song that goes, 'These *are* the good old days,'" Jane reflected. "You've got a house full of love. And I have…" She hesitated for a fraction of a second. "Stopgap." Her quick smile took the edge off the remark.

Luke caught her hands. "You have a lot more than that."

"Name three things."

He had no trouble coming up with an answer. "Two little girls next door and their pushy father."

"Who likes to hold hands in empty office suites," she murmured.

He'd like to hold much more than that. But as usual, his timing, not to mention his location, was completely off. Wendy Clark stuck her head in the door, and he stepped away quickly.

She'd just heard from a service club looking for a new project in Brea. "I told them they were sent from heaven," she announced happily.

Luke took that as a good omen. The clinic, which he already thought of informally as Annie's place, was off to a promising start.

JANE COULDN'T BELIEVE how many men asked her to dance.

On Friday, after a delicious dinner, she, Brooke and Renée had moved from the Anaheim restaurant's main area to the bar, which featured a deejay and a dance floor.

Renée attracted the usual flurry of attention. Brooke, always a charmer, waved away invitations, confiding to Jane that as she was still nursing her breasts felt uncomfortably heavy. Besides, she didn't feel right dancing with someone while Oliver stayed home with Marlene.

As for Jane, she'd have been satisfied with an invitation from a sedate older fellow. To her astonishment, a sharp young guy with multiple piercings put in his bid first.

"You're hot," he told her as they gyrated within hip-bumping range.

"You, too."

That marked the extent of their conversation, since no sooner had the music segued to another song than a second man cut in. More in Jane's age range, he sported a tight shirt, trendy jeans and a medley of tattoos.

"Sexy," he told her.

"You, too." She tried to look as if she meant it.

"No, you *most*." He grinned, revealing a gap in his teeth.

She'd barely finished the dance and sat down with Brooke when a third man, suave and graying at the temples, requested her company. Off they went, squeezing onto the packed floor. He shouted his name at her, but over the loud music Jane couldn't tell whether it was Harry, Larry or Cary.

Probably a made-up name anyway. He kept his left hand out of sight, perhaps hiding either a wedding ring or the telltale white strip where one belonged.

Why were these guys so intent on flirting with her? Curious, Jane glanced at her reflection in the mirror behind the bar.

Shimmering lights caught the blond strands Renée had woven into her hair that afternoon. Her makeup sparkled, too, and the cosmetician had plucked and shaded and shaped until Jane hardly recognized that sophisticated face as her own.

She whirled away, feeling the silky teal dress skim her figure. Sherry hadn't been able to attend tonight because she was babysitting Luke's girls, but she'd gone shopping with Jane and selected this flattering outfit as her gift.

Sherry had also insisted on new lingerie, including a bustline-boosting bra. "If you've got it, flaunt it, girl-friend," she'd observed with a grin.

Another whirl, and Jane checked the mirror again. Was that actual cleavage peeking from the deep vee of her neckline? Goodness. She'd never considered herself a slouch in the looks department, but she'd needed a makeover more than she'd realized.

The music stopped. "Gonna take a short break," the deejay announced. "I'll be back in five, folks."

"Why don't we go somewhere more private?" said Harry, Larry or Cary. Or possibly he'd said Terry.

"I'm with friends," Jane told him.

"They'll understand."

The overhead lights brightened enough for her to see

Brooke waving madly from across the room. "Afraid not." She might be blowing off the man of her dreams, Jane mused with a final glance at his silvering hair and bedroom eyes. But she doubted it. "Thanks, anyway."

"Your loss." With a shrug, he strolled off.

As she neared the table, she realized Brooke wasn't simply waving. She was holding up a cell phone.

"You've got a call." Her friend must have plucked it from Jane's purse, which sat open beside her. "From Luke."

Why would he be phoning? Jane pressed it to her ear, trying to block the buzz of voices in the room. "What's up?"

His deep voice came through clearly. "Sorry to disturb your birthday, but I've got two women being prepped for C-sections. I'm on my way into surgery—one's twins and they're early. The other patient's yours. She's in a lot of pain and I wondered if you could come in."

"Of course." Thank goodness she'd only had a small glass of wine with dinner, and that had been hours ago.

"Emergency?" Brooke inquired when Jane snapped her phone shut.

She explained the situation. "Can you do surgery in that dress?" Renée asked.

"I'll change at the hospital," Jane assured her.

"Put the dress on afterward," her friend advised. "Luke ought to see it."

She did look smokin' tonight, didn't she? Jane thought in amusement. Three men had told her so.

The wrong three men. Anyway, she had more important matters to deal with. A mother-to-be was counting on her.

DESPITE BEING BORN nearly a month early, the two little girls emitted lusty cries as soon as their lungs cleared. As he closed the mother's incision, Luke was pleased to hear that the twins weighed more than five pounds each.

"They can stay in the neonatal unit right here," one of the pediatricians told the parents. "No reason to transport them to Children's Hospital."

In the birthing suite, the nurses beamed with relief. Luke extended his congratulations to the new father, who thanked him distractedly. With a pair of infants and a convalescing wife to care for, the man had a lot on his plate.

Luke completed his stitching and exchanged a few reassuring words with the mother. She seemed happy, although tired and woozy from the anesthetic.

After cleaning up, he asked a nurse about Jane's surgery. "She delivered a little boy about ten minutes ago," the woman said.

"Is she still in the hospital?"

"I think she's changing."

"Thanks." It was nearly midnight. Too late to pick up the kids, who were sleeping at Sherry's house.

He called Jane and asked her to meet him in the doctors' lounge. He wanted to escort her to her car, and to apologize again for spoiling her birthday outing. Earlier, when he'd glimpsed her in green scrubs with a cap over her hair, her face had been flushed. Probably from dancing with her friends. Must have been a fun evening.

The lounge door opened and in stepped a stunning blonde in a blue-green dress that emphasized a curvaceous figure. As he was trying to figure out what to say, she regarded him with skeptical amusement. "Luke Van Dam, don't you recognize me?"

"Good Lord." Could that be Jane? "You look even more beautiful than usual."

"Quick recovery," she teased.

"The only thing I have to recover from is being dazzled," Luke shot back. "You did something fantastic with your hair."

"For the record, that wasn't my hair you were staring at," Jane returned. "Honestly, Luke, are you telling me that at this point in your career, you *still* don't know anatomy?"

He gave her a lazy smile, trying to disguise the eagerness radiating through his body. He knew his anatomy, all right. But he didn't know hers nearly well enough.

Her self-assured air wavered as she glanced down at her dress. "Do you think I'm overdoing it? Sherry swore it wasn't too revealing, but the way the men were staring at me…"

"Which men?"

"All of them."

He didn't like the sound of that. "I thought you were dancing with your friends."

"I was *sitting* with my friends. I was dancing with men," she corrected. "Luke, are you jealous?"

"Yes," he said.

"Really?"

"Why wouldn't I be?" he responded. "You're a knockout. And I feel protective of you. How dare those mashers ogle you?"

"I don't need protecting," she said.

"Every man wants to be a superhero to his woman," Luke told her.

"His woman?" she queried.

"It's late. And I'm feeling gallant." Then he remembered the small treat he'd bought for them to share. "If you aren't in a hurry, we could swing by the office and pick up the champagne I left there by mistake."

"Champagne?" she echoed.

"A thirty-fifth birthday calls for a toast," Luke said. "And I want to be the one to clink glasses with you."

"Sounds like a plan."

They rode the elevator to a lobby deserted at this hour. So there was no one to notice when Luke's arm slipped around Jane's waist.

His good friend had been transformed into a sizzling temptress. Tonight, if he had his way, he'd like to tempt her right back.

Chapter Eleven

In the medical suite, shadows sculpted the corridors and the counters loomed like outcroppings in some lunar landscape. Jane realized she had never before visited the place at night.

Luke's hand on her back guided her along the hall. "Seems a waste," he murmured, his breath tickling her ear.

"What does?" Her voice echoed.

"All this space and nobody using it half the time."

"Think we should sublet it?" she asked. "Although I can't imagine who'd work here after dark."

"Vampire doctors?"

"I'm not letting them anywhere near *my* A-positive blood."

He paused in the corridor, his thumb tracing the pulse of her throat. Heat radiated through Jane. "I didn't mention my other identity?" Luke teased.

She leaned into his warmth. "Don't forget, I've seen you in sunlight."

"And I've seen you in moonlight," he murmured in response. "You're bewitching."

His voice quivered into her heart. Bewitched. That was exactly how she felt.

"My office," he murmured.

"What?"

"That's where I left the champagne."

"I don't think we need champagne." Not with excitement effervescing through her veins.

"It's private." In the faint gleam of a security light, his eyes became fathomless pools.

Jane laughed.

"What?"

"Like this whole place isn't private?" She shook her head. "Okay, let's go get the champagne."

"I may have some disposable glasses, too," he said as they ventured farther into the darkness.

"Let's just inject it directly into our bloodstream."

"Is that legal?"

"Who cares?" she tossed back.

In his office, a soft glow seeped through the tilted blinds from the streetlights. Luke shut the door.

Close to him now, Jane heard his rapid breathing. Her own heart was beating so hard she imagined he could surely feel the vibrations.

A tiny voice inside tried to impose some restraint. Did she really want to do this? Oh, hell, yes.

Luke brushed back her hair, his gaze scorching across her face. Then he explored her lips with his until fire blossomed within her and they gripped each other with pure liquid longing.

Jane eased open Luke's jacket and ran her palm across the T-shirt beneath. A groan ripped from him.

She could hardly believe she was really here, caressing and arousing him. At the same time, she couldn't imagine why she'd ever given this up.

Her body ached for him, but he took his time stroking her, bringing her nipples to hard points through the silky fabric and kissing her again, deeply. Jane gripped him, thrilled by the power rippling in his muscles.

When Luke eased behind her and lowered her zipper, she felt a moment of self-consciousness. She forgot it as he lifted the curls from her nape, and the flick of his tongue on her spine sent hunger spiraling through her.

He swung her carefully around and fingered the dainty lingerie. Lifting the bra to expose her breasts, he knelt and touched them with his tongue.

Jane couldn't bear to wait another moment. Fiercely, she tugged at his clothes until his T-shirt and slacks found their way to the floor along with her lacy panties. "I want this," he whispered. "I've been wanting this forever."

"I want it *now*," Jane answered.

"That works for me," he teased, his voice thick with desire.

Luke retrieved a condom—in plentiful supply on these premises—and then they were on the couch, nuzzling and seeking. When his hardness slid inside her, Jane thought she might soar right through the roof. Thank heaven for his anchoring weight and the ferocity of his thrusts.

She lifted herself to kiss his bare chest and relished his taut moan. "Not so fast," Luke whispered. "Let's make this last."

But she couldn't hold back, and neither could he. Their movements quickened, and then, in a moment of utter joy, they fused, purifying like ore into gold. Jane arched against him and shudders racked them both.

A shout burst from his throat, primal and joyous.

"Unbelievable," he managed to say, and sank down, squeezing against her in the narrow space.

Jane lay cocooned in his embrace. She could see now that she'd craved this moment since she caught sight of him at the hospital. But once wasn't enough. Not nearly enough.

"Exactly how tired are you?" she whispered.

"Allow me to demonstrate," he murmured, and proceeded to rise to new heights. In every sense.

"DID YOU KNOW that when you get aroused, your irises turn purple?" Jane asked afterward as they lay gazing into each other's eyes.

Deliciously sated, Luke inhaled the scent of her perfume tinged with antiseptic. "How can you tell in this light?"

"I have great night vision."

Shifting position, he discovered she was cutting off the blood flow in his leg. Much as he hated to disturb this peaceful moment, they ought to get moving. "Your place or mine?"

She sighed. "If one of us leaves the other's house in the morning, somebody'll see. It'll be all over the neighborhood."

"We could sleep in until really late."

"What about collecting the girls?"

He'd forgotten about them. How was that possible? A function of the one-track male libido, he supposed. "You suppose they might sleep late, too?"

"Not a chance." She wriggled from his grasp. Wincing, Luke untangled his legs and let her up.

What a lovely picture she made, gloriously nude,

hair haloing her face, eyes shining with slaked lust. Luke sure hoped it was slaked, because he couldn't do much more about it for a while.

At least an hour. By then, unfortunately, she'd be gone.

He refused to be satisfied with just a few stolen moments. They needed to work out a way to spend more time together, especially on those rare occasions when the girls weren't home.

"Maybe we ought to let the neighbors wag their jaws and get used to us," he suggested.

"You may not feel that way after you've lived here longer," Jane warned. "I don't mean that they rule my life or anything."

"Don't they?" He didn't intend to needle her. Still, Luke objected to the repressive power of gossip.

Jane retrieved her panties from where they'd dropped. The woman sure had great taste in underwear, he reflected as she slipped them into place.

"Having a baby on my own isn't exactly old-fashioned behavior, is it? I'll do what feels right to me, gossip be damned," she said. "But folks have long memories and it's a close-knit community."

Luke scooped up his T-shirt. "Why would I worry about people's long memories? It's not as if I'm going to be around here forever."

With her dress halfway on, Jane paused. From her startled expression, he gathered he'd said the wrong thing. Did she expect him to stay here permanently? That had never been Luke's plan.

"You sound as if you're already planning your next career move," Jane said edgily.

"Of course I am. Sean's only going to be gone for a

year." Luke pulled on the T-shirt. "That doesn't mean you and I have to lose contact."

"What about Zoey? She's making friends and getting comfortable at a school," she said. "And you seemed all gung ho about this Annie Raft clinic. Who's going to run that?"

He had to admit, he hadn't worked out all the logistics. "I'm not planning to flee the moment the clock strikes midnight. But I never intended to run the clinic myself. My goal is to help get it off the ground organizationally and financially. Of course I'll donate my time as long as I'm in the area."

"Until you take off for a better job halfway across the country." Her dress zippered up, Jane searched around the floor for something.

He didn't see why she was worrying about an event so far in the future. "There are a lot of outstanding hospitals within a two-hour radius of here. But tonight belongs to us, so let's ignore the tongue-wagging neighbors. You and I should maximize every minute we can spend together."

She stared at him as if he'd insulted her. "Maximize our time? How romantic!"

"Jane, why are we fighting?"

"Because…because I should have known better!" she flared. "Because you're acting like your old self again."

"And that's bad?"

She plopped onto a chair and pulled on her stockings. "Oh, shoot."

"What?"

"I ripped them." She yanked them off and stuck them in her purse. Careful not to leave them in the trash where a curious employee might spot them, Luke mused.

"You're my best friend," he said. "And my lover. I want to keep it that way."

"And I want to go home." She stuck her feet into her shoes and headed for the exit.

He accompanied her out. Not until he was alone in his car, trailing her back to Harmony Circle, did Luke realize he'd forgotten the champagne.

Well, he didn't feel much like celebrating anymore, anyway.

JANE COULDN'T BELIEVE she'd made the same mistake all over again. Tumbled for Luke, only to discover that he was still the same love-'em-and-leave-'em type he'd been in med school.

Okay, maybe that was unfair. He'd proposed they remain lovers. But only until a better job beckoned.

Jane deserved more. Not that she expected him to promise her forever after one night. But she'd assumed—foolishly, she could see now—that there were good reasons for him staying here. The girls' circle of friends, the proposed clinic, the way he enjoyed the neighborhood...

Long-distance relationships didn't foster intimacy. So what if he wanted to remain her now-and-then lover? She needed a man she could count on, not some guy who blew into town when it suited his schedule.

At home, she laid her new dress over a chair to take to the dry cleaner's. After tossing her panty hose in the trash, she pulled on her favorite baggy T-shirt and stared at her image in the mirror.

The hair still looked great. And so, she concluded defiantly, did she.

You are a special person. Tonight you wowed a bunch of guys in a bar and performed surgery that saved a baby's life. You ripped the pants off Luke Van Dam and experienced moments of nirvana.

And now, back to reality.

"What did I expect, anyway?" she asked Stopgap, who sat panting at her feet. "True love, from Luke? He wouldn't know it if it bit him. Which isn't a bad idea. How'd you like to take a nip out of him tomorrow?"

The spaniel had nothing to say on the subject.

The worst part, Jane mused as she went downstairs for ice cream, was that she couldn't stay angry at the man. What a thrill it had been, to feel his desire for her overwhelm his self-control. For a few incredibly sweet moments, she'd swept him away. He'd done the same for her. She'd climaxed twice and one of those might have been a double.

Yet at some level, she should have seen this coming. Luke had always gone slip-sliding out of the picture whenever a relationship grew intense. True, he'd stuck by Pauline when she got pregnant, but that had been for Zoey's sake. What was wrong with the man?

"Mocha chocolate. Vanilla bean. Praline caramel." Jane read the labels in the freezer. "Since it's my birthday, I'll have all three."

She tossed a few doggie treats into Stopgap's bowl and ate at the table with her feet propped on a chair. Delicious. This was *almost* the best part of the evening.

Not quite. Oh, heck. Not even *nearly* quite.

What she ought to do, Jane concluded, was to take the lemons life handed her and make a lemon meringue pie. She'd been on a collision course with her own weakness for Luke ever since he turned up in Brea, and maybe, subconsciously, before that. Now that she'd gone the distance with him and discovered that it led nowhere, she could move on.

Could, should and would.

She'd always longed to establish a real home, the kind she'd missed out on growing up. The kind that came with two loving parents and at least one child. Passion ought to be part of that, but if her libido insisted on being hung up on Luke, she'd teach it a lesson by finding another man who'd suit her just as well. A man who'd stick around, even if that meant searching for someone whose quiet passion would thrill her in a different way.

The hell with it! The problem with thinking so much was that it distracted her from the ice cream.

Jane scooped out another serving and settled back to indulge.

Chapter Twelve

From the moment Luke awoke on Saturday morning, he couldn't stop thinking about Jane. About how incredibly right it had felt to be inside her. About their quarrel, which they should have been able to resolve like reasonable adults.

He wished more than ever that they'd spent the night together. He'd have loved to see the morning light on her face. Why did she have to be so stubborn?

Around eight o'clock, he collected the girls from Sherry's house. Zoey was bubbling over with energy, so he suggested a swim at the pool, where she played with friends while Tina splashed around with Luke.

A couple of attractive women lounging poolside offered to share their sunscreen and made a fuss over the baby, while sneaking glances at Luke. His own gaze kept straying toward the sidewalk in the hope that Jane might appear.

Now, after lunch, the girls were spending some quiet time. He'd left Zoey reading a picture book in her room while Tina napped in her bassinet. Luke valued the chance to check his e-mail without interruption.

Today, this father business had been going smoothly. Thank goodness he got the occasional break from the ongoing drama.

The phone rang.

Although he'd finished his stint on call, Luke braced for the possibility of an emergency. Instead, he heard his ex-wife's gleeful voice saying his name as glasses clinked somewhere near her.

She was in Las Vegas, he recalled. Probably having a late breakfast after last night's performance. He glanced at his watch. A very late breakfast.

"Luke!" she repeated, and giggled.

Those weren't juice glasses, he surmised. Very likely, she'd never even gone to bed last night. "What's going on, Pauline?"

"Izzy got a contact." At least, that's what he thought she said, but it made no sense.

"What?"

"Hold on." She moved to a quieter area where the background noise faded. "A2Zee got a recording contract."

"Congratulations." A2Zee was the band cofounded by her boyfriend, Jason Zuniga. He'd joined his initial *Z* to a fellow guitarist's *A*, for Allenby or Alanon or something.

"We've been celebrating all night." She snorted. "And guess what? This morning, we got married."

Luke took a moment to absorb the news. His ex-wife was now Jason's. Well, good for them. But what was this going to mean to Zoey? Pauline still hadn't bothered to visit. How could she think intermittent phone conversations were enough for a seven-year-old? "Zoey's missed you."

"I'll come see her next week."

"She isn't a toy that you can ignore when you get bored with her," he snapped.

"You were the one who insisted she stay with you!" Before he could react to this unfair barb, Pauline went on. "Jason and I deserve a few days to ourselves. It's our honeymoon."

Luke turned at a noise from the hall. It was Zoey. In this small cottage, she couldn't have helped overhearing his end of the conversation. "Is that Mom?"

He nodded. "Your daughter's here," he informed his ex-wife. "I'll let you tell her the news." He handed over the phone.

For the next few minutes, Zoey listened and pleaded. "I miss you, Mommy," and "How soon is soon?"

The pain in her voice tore at Luke. Tina apparently picked up on it, too, because she started wailing for reassurance. He scooped the squalling infant from the bassinet. So much for a break from the drama.

Zoey was now in tears. "I have to be your flower girl. Get married again!" she sobbed to her mother. A moment later, lip quivering, his daughter thrust the phone at Luke.

He took it grimly. "Yes?"

"I can't deal with her tantrum," Pauline told him. "I haven't even called my mother yet."

"That wasn't a tantrum. It was an honest reaction."

Against his shoulder and close to the phone, Tina let out a shriek. "Jeez, my ear!" Pauline griped. "Is that the baby you rescued? She's got a set of lungs on her. Well, I've got to go. Kiss Zoey for me."

He hung up, too angry to answer. The sight of his daughter's stricken face wrenched at Luke even harder. He wished he could fix this for her, but that was beyond him.

"Your mom loves you," he told her in a weak attempt at reassurance. *Sure she does, in her own selfish way.*

"I want to be her flower girl," the little girl whimpered. "I hate Jason. Why can't she marry you?"

"We tried and it didn't work." Tina, whose wriggling had subsided, emitted a large grunt. Uh-oh. "I'm sorry. Diaper duty."

"You always put her first," Zoey complained. "I hate her."

"You don't mean that."

She glared at him.

"We'll talk in a minute." Luke felt her fury follow him out of the room.

Handling two children was tough enough under normal circumstances. He hadn't considered how he'd manage if either faced a crisis.

From the front of the house, he registered the scrape of the door. "Zoey! Where are you going?"

"To help Jane garden. It's Saturday. I promised." The door slammed behind her.

Luke cursed under his breath. This might be a safe neighborhood, but he'd have preferred to take her next door himself. Instead, he had to finish changing Tina.

Afterward, he called Jane. "She's here," his neighbor confirmed. "We're out in the yard. She said you were okay with this."

"Did she mention her mother?"

"We're having that discussion right now" was the wry response. "This is a tough one."

"It sure is," he admitted. "I suppose the upside is that Pauline probably won't object to her staying with me permanently, but this is terribly hard on Zoey."

"Stay calm. She'll take her cue from you," Jane replied. "Listen, as soon as we finish planting lettuce, we'll wash up. Why don't you come over. I'm sure she'd like to show you what we've been doing."

"We'll be there."

As he clicked off, he noted that she hadn't said a word about last night. Well, he wasn't going to let their relationship deteriorate the way it had ten years ago. They'd find the right balance for them both.

The phone rang. He thought she was calling back to ask him something else, until he checked the display.

Delilah Lincoln. A few days earlier, the social worker had called to discuss starting the home-study process, but that wasn't scheduled for several weeks.

"Sorry to bother you on the weekend, Doctor," she said after they exchanged hellos.

"Is everything all right?"

"There's a problem with Mrs. Raft."

Luke gritted his teeth. Although Annie's mother had threatened to hire a lawyer, he'd heard nothing further about that.

His gaze flew to the little girl, who, freshly changed, was rolling on the carpet with her teddy bear. No way would he betray Annie's trust by turning her over to that woman.

Yet if a judge had ruled against him, he might have no choice. "What's happened?" he asked, and waited impatiently for her to tell him.

Zoey TROMPED into the house behind Jane. "I can't wait to eat the lettuce."

"We just sowed the seeds," Jane pointed out. "The

plants won't be big enough to eat for a couple of months. Gardening takes patience."

"I hate patience."

"You hate everything today." She'd listened to a litany of complaints from the grumpy child.

Zoey shook her head. "I don't hate you."

"I'm glad of that."

From his resting place on the floor, Stopgap whined.

"Or you," Zoey assured him.

They went into the bathroom, with the dog padding behind. As she waited while the girl washed her face and hands, Jane's thoughts turned to Pauline's marriage. Apparently the woman hadn't given a second thought to how her daughter might feel about being excluded from the ceremony.

As a physician, Jane understood that not all women fully adjusted to motherhood, especially after an unplanned pregnancy. But if she had a little girl like this, she'd battle demons and ogres before she let anything separate them. Or hurt her daughter the way Zoey obviously was now.

The doorbell rang. "That's probably your dad. I'll get it. You okay here on your own?"

The little girl nodded. Stopgap let out a sharp bark, as if agreeing.

Jane found Luke on the porch. The sheer physicality of the man slammed into her as she took in the warmth of his gaze and the strength of his arms holding the baby against one shoulder.

She'd vowed to seek satisfaction elsewhere. How exactly was she supposed to do that when just being around him shredded her resistance?

"Is Zoey holding up okay?" he asked.

She moved aside to let him in. "She's crabby but otherwise intact."

He stepped into the living room. "I feel awful for her. There ought to be something I can do. Instead, I wasn't even there for her, because I had to take care of Tina."

"It goes with the territory," Jane said, although she had to admit she'd never actually been in that situation.

"It's rotten timing all around. But I can't blame that. I'm their dad. I have to do what's best for my children." Luke seemed to be muttering as much to himself as to Jane.

"What're you talking about?"

"There's something else.... Where *is* Zoey?"

"Hold on. I'll check." Jane found the little girl in the den, playing with the dog. "Zoey, your dad and I have some grown-up business to discuss. Would you like to watch TV with Stopgap?"

"Sure."

She found a cartoon channel for Zoey and rejoined Luke in the living room. "What's up?"

He dandled the baby on his knee. "Annie's mother and her boyfriend got busted for drugs. They were selling the stuff right out of the apartment."

"That's awful." On the other hand, she realized, this improved the picture. "No court will give her custody after this."

"Exactly." His lips quirked but didn't quite form a smile. "I won't have to fight to keep Tina away from her grandmother. The problem is, now that Brenda's out of the picture, I have to wonder if I'm being fair to Tina. Or to Zoey, either."

"What do you mean?" The distress in his voice troubled Jane.

The baby began squirming, so he set her on the carpet. "Zoey deserves more attention than I've been able to give her. Pauline's marriage is going to stress out Zoey for a long time. The situation's far from ideal for Tina, either. She's practically growing up in day care."

Sitting on the floor beside the baby, Jane fingered a tuft of blond hair. "You can't be thinking of giving her up. With her mother out of the picture, what other relatives does she have?"

"None, apparently. Certainly none that Annie trusted," Luke admitted. "But when she appointed me guardian, she made it my responsibility to protect her child's best interests. If she'd be better off with the right adoptive parents, then I owe it to her to make that choice."

Tina climbed on Jane's lap. Snuggling the little girl, Jane felt a surge of fierce protectiveness. "She belongs here, with you." *And me.*

His anguished gaze fell on the tot's upturned face. "I adore her, but I don't believe she's fully bonded with me yet. She's only been with me just over a week. If I can't in all fairness keep her, I should give her up soon."

"No, you shouldn't," Jane flared. "You've been coping amazingly well. Tina's flourishing. Both girls are."

Luke shook his head. "I'm barely hanging on as a single father. When Zoey had her meltdown, I was too busy with the baby to pay attention. She ran out the door before I could stop her. What if she *hadn't* simply come to your place?"

Was he really putting his daughters' interest first, or

dodging yet another relationship? Jane bit her lip, regretting the ugly thought. After all, she was hardly an objective observer. *I guess I am still a little angry with him about last night.*

He obviously needed a break. "Here's what you're going to do right now," Jane announced. "Leave Tina with me. Spend the day with Zoey, showing her how much she means to you. Having a little space should help clear your head."

He gave her a grateful look. "Are you sure you don't mind?"

"We'll make an outing of it, with Stopgap." Tina ought to enjoy the walk, and so would Jane.

He reached for her hand to help her to her feet. And held on to it. "I don't like the way we left things last night. You and I are…"

"…better off as friends," she responded as pleasantly as she could. "Luke, we want very different things out of life."

"I'm sorry I can't fulfill my ambitions in a small-town practice," he said sadly. "Jane, let's not lose each other again. I don't see why we have to."

Into her mind flashed a memory from their fourth year of residency. When a multicar pileup overloaded the hospital's emergency room with patients too critical to transport to other facilities, they'd been stretched almost beyond their abilities.

Upset at the sight of so much suffering, Jane had concentrated on simply following the resident doctors' directions. Luke, though, had been galvanized. It was he, not an intern or resident, who'd spotted a pregnant woman about to go into shock from internal bleeding. His insistence that she receive priority treatment had probably saved her life and that of her baby.

Much as the man was good at providing routine care, he thrived on adrenaline. He couldn't give that up, and, after all, hadn't they become physicians to help people as best they could? He simply had different skills, and a different personality, than Jane.

Unfortunately, that meant he had to disappoint some people, including her. And maybe Tina, as well. But that remained to be seen.

"I'm sorry, too," Jane told him. "And you aren't exactly losing me." To her annoyance, her voice caught. "Oh, heck. Go have fun with your daughter."

He gave her hand a squeeze before releasing it. "I'm not giving up that easily."

She left that argument for later. Not much later, though. Since the options were getting her heart broken in a few months or years, or getting it broken now, she chose now.

The idea of a day with Dad cheered Zoey, and soon they were off, laughing together. After collecting the stroller from Luke's house, Jane set out with Tina and Stopgap. On this sunny spring day, flower beds along Harmony Road burst with calla lilies, poppies, daisies and pansies, while the breeze carried the briny tang of the sea from fifteen miles away.

As she walked, Jane was startled to see a small green parrot flash onto a low-growing palm not more than a dozen feet away. She'd heard that escaped parrots flourished in Orange County, but she had never seen any.

"Parrot," she told Tina. "Isn't it beautiful?"

The little girl reached toward the colorful bird,

although it was clearly too far away to touch. Jane made out a white chest and a bit of orange fluff above the beak. Cocking its head, it uttered an inquiring croak.

Fearlessly, Tina squawked back. The bird ruffled its feathers and screeched again before flashing away in a blur of green.

"Guess you two are on the same wavelength," Jane told the baby.

What a precious moment, and what a shame that Tina's mom wasn't here to witness it, Jane thought as she continued her stroll. At least Annie's love had protected her child by guiding her to Luke.

Was he right to relinquish her? If he couldn't be dissuaded, if someone other than him was going to raise her, it ought to be Jane.

The moment the idea struck her, she recognized it as the perfect, logical, loving solution. But he'd said before that he believed children deserved two parents. Would that stubborn man insist on finding a married couple?

Heading down the far side of Harmony Road, she passed Bart's place. At the house next door, whose wealthy owners had left it vacant for the time being, he was fertilizing a white rosebush. The absentee couple allowed Bart to experiment with plantings in exchange for taking care of their yard.

"Great blooms," she said. "You're a wizard."

He shut off the sprayer. "You found a baby. Congratulations!"

"What? No," Jane said in confusion.

"Sorry." Bart's sun-weathered forehead formed a crease. "I heard you were going to adopt." He took a closer look. "Oh, it's Tina. How're you doing, cutie?"

"I'm babysitting." Jane made a mental note to be *much* more careful what she said around the Foxes.

"That's too bad. I mean, it's good. Of you. To babysit." Bart avoided any more verbal stumbling by crouching to scratch Stopgap's ears.

"I wish she *were* mine," Jane burst out.

"Why don't you come on in for a cup of tea," Bart said. "I've got cookies, too."

In the four years she'd lived in Harmony Circle, this was the first time he'd invited her to his place. "I'd enjoy that."

They entered the kitchen through the back. Instead of the scruffy bachelor-pad decor Jane had expected, custom oak cabinetry and a curving, beautifully designed dinette set met her gaze. "Did you make these yourself?"

"Yep. Grew the peppermint for the tea, too." With a shy smile, Bart put water on to boil.

After downing a lemon cookie, Tina enjoyed rolling on the polished wooden floor, with Stopgap lounging close by. Bart brought in a chunky maple car for her to play with. "It's left from a bunch I carved for my nieces and nephews."

"How many do you have?"

"I lost count. The more the merrier." Warmth shone from him.

Looking on Bart as a casual friend, she'd never really noticed him much before, Jane thought. Yet from the glances he was casting her way, he'd obviously noticed *her*. That reminded her of the admiring remarks he'd made to Luke when the men were alone.

Over an aromatic cup of tea, she told him about Tina's grandmother and the possibility that Luke might seek a new home for the girl. "At one level, I understand his concerns. But what a shame."

"He'd let this sweetheart go, if he found the right couple?" Bart watched Tina wave the wooden car in the air. "That'd be a real loss."

"It kills me to think of strangers getting her," Jane agreed.

"If he *is* looking for a family…" Breaking off, Bart got a strange look on his face.

"What?" Jane pressed.

He studied her for a long moment, and then words spilled out. "Once in my life, I let something precious slip through my fingers because I didn't react fast enough. Guess I was scared to take a chance. Well, not this time. Jane, you're a beautiful woman and you could do better than me, but I'd love if you were willing to make a leap of faith."

She didn't follow his train of thought. "What do you mean?"

"Let's get married." Excitement glimmered in his cornflower-blue eyes.

He was proposing? How utterly unexpected. "Because of Tina?"

"She gave me the idea, or maybe the courage to ask you," he admitted. "But I've been thinking about this for a while. I suppose I should have done the whole dating thing, but getting to know each other informally seemed more natural."

They *had* spent a lot of time together, Jane realized, laying out and cultivating her garden, reviewing the creative plantings he'd installed on his neighbor's property and, in the process, discussing whatever else came into their minds. But she'd never twigged to the fact that Bart considered this a courtship. How could she have been so oblivious?

"Even if it doesn't work out with Tina, we could still have a child," Bart continued. "Jane, being around you makes life fun. I'd enjoy sharing a pregnancy with you, if that's what you want. I know I've caught you off guard, and I apologize, but we could create a wonderful home together. Please don't say no."

At the moment, she couldn't say anything at all. He'd startled her speechless.

Her practical nature clamored that this was what she'd sought, a loving man who shared her values, who wouldn't go haring off in search of glory and who'd always be there for her. If Luke hadn't returned to Brea, she'd probably have accepted Bart's proposal without reservation.

Yet Luke *had* returned. And in his arms, she'd rediscovered a joy she'd never experienced with anyone else. How high a value did she place on passion? Enough to sustain her during long separations, or comfort her if she lost him entirely?

What a dilemma, and what a life-changing choice. Jane knew better than to rush into a decision. "I hope it's all right if I take a few days to consider."

"Sure." Bart studied her tensely. "Jane, you aren't just letting me down easy, are you?"

"Absolutely not." What kind of cruel woman would do that? "I thoroughly enjoy our friendship, but marriage is a huge step. I have to be sure."

He nodded. "I'd expect nothing less of you." When she got to her feet, Bart knelt to put Tina in the stroller, handling the baby tenderly and confidently. He must have gained experience with those nieces and nephews.

Bart *was* a good man, and he'd make a terrific husband. For someone.

Jane left in a daze. Dreams didn't always come true the way you expected, but she wasn't about to dismiss this opportunity, not by a long shot.

Chapter Thirteen

By Monday, Luke figured Zoey was over the worst of her moodiness. They'd spent hours at her favorite park on Saturday, and on Sunday, with Tina in tow, they'd paid a visit to Hetty.

She'd engulfed her granddaughter in a hug and presented her with a charm bracelet, "Just like I used to wear when I was your age." To Tina, Hetty had kindly given a terry-cloth bunny.

That night, Luke taught Zoey a simple card game. She didn't seem to mind when he got distracted once or twice by the baby's antics.

Perhaps they'd weathered this storm and he could keep both girls. Feeling as if he'd been granted parole from a prison sentence, Luke was bursting with energy when he and Jane met Wendy Clark in her office during their lunch break on Tuesday.

"I've got our grant writer working on a couple of proposals," the administrator told them. "She feels this project is very viable if we can get the community involved."

Luke reported on the progress he'd made. "I put in calls to a couple of colleagues around here. They all agreed to refer patients, and one said she could donate one afternoon a month. They'll help spread the word, as well."

He'd also e-mailed Sean, who'd responded with enthusiasm about picking up the ball after Luke's departure. However, it seemed premature to mention his long-term plans to Wendy, so he left that point for later.

Jane had something to contribute, as well. "One of my patients is a counselor with the local school district. When I mentioned the clinic to her, she said they're looking for ways to encourage pregnant girls not to drop out. Maybe we can involve the school system, both to identify patients and for partial funding."

"That's a great idea," Luke told her, pleased by her initiative.

"It's my project too, remember," she told him.

"Excellent." Wendy tapped her pen on a pad. "I have to admit, this is a bit less high-tech than some of the programs I'd like to institute here, but it will fill a need and provide great outreach."

"What sort of projects?" This was the first Luke had heard on that subject.

"We're not making the best use of our MRI scanner, for example." Magnetic resonance imaging devices could cost millions of dollars but were invaluable in cancer diagnosis and treatment. "Compared to City of Hope and St. Jude, our cancer treatment center is on the small side, so we've missed out on some exciting projects. Any ideas on that score, either of you?"

Luke shook his head. "I'll keep my eyes open, now that I'm aware of your interest." He did his best to keep up with cutting-edge research through medical journals and Web sites. Plus he planned to renew his contacts at a medical conference to be held in Anaheim next fall.

"It's not exactly my line of interest, but if I stumble across anything, I'll pass it along," Jane agreed.

Afterward, as they headed back to the office, he thanked her again for giving him time alone with Zoey on Saturday. "It made a world of difference."

"Any more thoughts regarding Tina?" Her casual tone struck him as slightly forced.

Luke stopped himself from blurting that he might not have to give her up after all. If he'd learned anything from his parenting experiences these past weeks, it was to expect the unexpected. "We're all getting along for the moment. I'm hoping for the best."

"Me, too," she said.

He noticed that she kept more distance between them than usual, and only met his eyes when necessary. "Jane, please don't pull away like you did last time."

"What last time?" Then she got it. "You mean ten years ago? Luke, that's ancient history."

"Yet we seem doomed to repeat it," he said grimly.

"We're not repeating anything," Jane responded as they cut behind the building toward the rear entrance. "Luke, we're simply both being true to ourselves."

"And that puts us on a collision course?" He slowed his stride to narrow the space between them.

"Collision course? Hardly. I'd say we were on a trajectory that's intersected a few times and then shot us off in different directions."

"I don't think a trajectory usually comes with all those contortions," he responded.

"If you tell me 'trajectory' was another of your vocabulary words, I'll smack you!" she responded, lengthening her stride.

Luke flinched. "I just like kidding around with you, that's all."

Jane glanced toward him, her expression softening. "I guess I'm a little preoccupied. Not much sense of humor these days."

"The baby business?" He hadn't heard any further mention of her plans to conceive on her own.

"Not exactly." She managed a tight smile. "I'm considering my options, that's all. And I'm delighted that things are going well with the girls. I hope it stays that way."

"So do I." He managed to beat her to the door, and held it as she went inside.

What options did she mean? The appearance of Pam Ortiz with files in hand forestalled further questions.

That afternoon, Wendy e-mailed that a local church was interested in providing volunteers to help staff the clinic. Buoyed by the news, Luke arrived at Maryam's after work. "How'd things go today?"

The day-care provider held up a plastic bag filled with stuffing and fabric. Puzzled, Luke peered closer until he recognized the bits of terry cloth as remnants of Tina's new bunny. Judging by the clean cuts, this toy had been cut to bits.

"Zoey did that?" he asked in dismay. "Any idea what set her off?"

"Tina's teething, so she's been fussier than usual. I guess her screeching got on Zoey's nerves." Maryam handed him the bag. "I found her and this behind the couch. It's amazing what a determined child can do with a pair of blunt-tipped scissors."

The implications worried Luke far beyond the loss of a stuffed animal. "You don't suppose she would hurt the baby, do you?"

"I can't be sure," Maryam said. "Since she's too young to fully understand the consequences of her actions, I've been careful not to leave them alone."

Heavyhearted, Luke greeted the girls and took them home. He supposed he ought to scold Zoey, but that might make her resent the baby even more.

Mentally, he ran through the steps he would advise a patient to take in such a situation. Although he wasn't a pediatrician, women sometimes asked his advice on family matters.

First, consult a counselor. He'd been planning to do that, to help Zoey deal with her reaction to Pauline's remarriage. But for all its merits, counseling wasn't a magic cure-all.

Second, spend time with each girl alone. How exactly did a single parent manage that on a daily basis?

Third, resolve any underlying issues of your own. As far as Luke knew, his only problem was getting custody of Zoey, which might be resolved now anyway. Okay, there was also his relationship with Jane, but she'd been helping with the girls, not hindering.

His spirits sank at the prospect that loomed ahead. Yet in light of his concerns for Tina's safety, what choice did he have but to find her a new, permanent home? He'd have to discuss the matter with Ms. Lincoln.

After dinner, both girls seemed subdued. Zoey kept shooting sideways glances at him, apparently expecting a reaction to her destructive behavior. She must have seen him with the bagged remnants of Tina's bunny.

At bedtime, after he read to her, Zoey climbed into his lap and hugged him. "I love you, Daddy."

"I love you, too, pumpkin." He tried in vain to hide the sadness in his voice.

She kept checking his face anxiously as she climbed back into bed. He yearned to reassure her, but his emotions refused to settle.

He turned out the lights and went in to see Tina. The baby sat in the crib, hugging her favorite bear.

"Da-da!" she greeted him.

Luke's heart expanded. Was she calling him Daddy?

He couldn't resist picking her up. With a happy coo, Tina threw her arms around his neck, her hair tickling his ear. The sensation sent Luke's mind back to the delivery room, when his first glimpse of Annie's baby had been her little head pushing into view with a tuft of hair plastered to the scalp.

Minutes later, cradling the baby, the new mom had regarded him with wonder. "I never did anything worthwhile in my whole life," she'd said. "Until now."

When he'd visited her hospital room the next day, she'd said, "I'd give my life for this baby. That's not like me! How could I change so fast?"

"You've become a mother," he'd told her.

"Guess that must be it," Annie had said. "And I'm going to be a good one."

She'd kept her word. Despite living completely in the moment, she'd looked far enough ahead to make out a will that safeguarded her daughter.

She wasn't around any longer to protect her little girl, Luke thought. He had to do it for her—and he would.

The sight of the plastic bag of bunny remnants

banished his misgivings. He only hoped it wouldn't take too long to identify a family he could recommend to Ms. Lincoln.

MORE THAN ONCE over the years, Jane had experienced a strong desire to wring Luke's neck. There'd been, for example, the postmidnight study session when, while all around him quizzed each other about metabolic disorders, he'd fallen asleep and snored loudly. The next day, he'd received the highest test score of any of them.

That, of course, was mere annoyance compared to how she'd felt at his cavalier declaration, after they made love last week, that he was determined to move on after Sean's return. Still, at least he'd simply been running true to type.

But on Wednesday, Jane got so mad she couldn't even speak to her partner. She'd just returned from lunch when he stopped by her office to say that he'd made an appointment to talk to attorney Tess Phipps to discuss finding an adoptive family for Tina. He hadn't wanted to bother Jane, he said, but she read the truth in his eyes. He'd settled on a course of action and hadn't asked her opinion because he already knew she disapproved. For heaven's sake, only yesterday he'd said the girls were getting along.

She didn't want to confront him at work. She was far too angry to be rational, anyway. If he had resolved to give up the baby, he ought to let her adopt. Had the thought even occurred to him? Well, if it hadn't, she'd make her case...once she calmed down.

As for Bart's proposal, her rational mind had been warring with her emotions since Saturday. She needed friendly advice to help her put things into perspective.

To that end, she fired off an e-mail inviting Brooke and Renée to a council of war but didn't specify the topic.

Mystified but supportive, they arrived at her house at seven o'clock that night, Renée carrying a bottle of wine and Brooke toting Marlene and a portable crib. "Oliver's out showing real estate," the young mother explained.

"Let's set that up in the corner." Jane bustled around with the crib.

"What's going on?" Renée sprawled in an armchair with a glass of red wine, apparently unconcerned about spilling any on her tailored slacks and silk shirt.

"You said it was urgent." Brooke smoothed her embroidered blouse over the baggy jeans that accommodated her full, postbaby figure.

They were the perfect advisers, Jane decided: Renée cool and independent, Brooke impulsive and loving. If these women couldn't help her, no one could.

"It's about Luke," she said.

"I figured." Renée sipped her wine. "That man's trouble. In a totally smokin' way."

"That's not what I meant." Jane collected her thoughts. "It's about what he's planning to do with Tina."

That got their attention. She proceeded to outline the story so far, omitting only the lovemaking, which she still hadn't mentioned to anyone. When she came to Bart's proposal, Brooke's eyes widened. "I never pictured him as a romantic."

"He's more the slow-burning type," Jane conceded. "But I got the feeling there are strong emotions underneath that cool surface."

"What about sex?" Renée asked.

"What about it?"

"Have you slept with him?"

Jane was trying to decide how much to reveal about her night with Luke, when she registered that her friend meant Bart. "Not everybody jumps between the sheets before they get married," she said defensively. "Hey, I'm confused about this. That's why I need your input."

"Take him for a test drive," Renée advised.

"He's not a car!"

"More of a utility vehicle, if you ask me. In the nicest sense," the hairdresser observed.

Brooke glanced over from where she knelt dangling a toy to amuse Marly. "I think this engagement is a good idea."

"You do?" Jane refrained from pointing out that she and Bart weren't actually engaged…yet.

Renée propped her feet atop the ottoman. "Why on earth?"

"It might kick-start Luke into figuring out how much he's throwing away," Brooke explained. "He's obviously crazy about Jane."

"I've noticed that, too." Renée took another sip.

The observation gave Jane pause. Then she reflected that her friends didn't know the man the way she did.

"I'm not interested in pushing him into anything," she said. "Luke and I want fundamentally different things from life." Seeing their skeptical expressions, she added, "He's already trying to figure out which major medical center he'll join for his next staff position. He's only sticking around here to do Sean a favor."

"That isn't a fundamentally different thing," Renée said. "That's a job change. Why can't *you* work at a major medical center, too?"

Much as she loved Harmony Circle, Jane knew she'd leave if the right circumstances presented themselves. "If we were committed to each other, I'm sure we'd work something out," she conceded. "But I've seen no indication he *wants* that."

"Call him," Renée said. "Go over there."

"And say what?"

"Tell him you're planning to marry Bart. That ought to shake him out of his complacency."

"I haven't made any such decision. And I refuse to manipulate him," Jane declared.

"Quit worrying about strategy," Brooke put in. "Your goal is to get Tina, right? Lay your cards on the table. What've you got to lose?"

Renée nodded. "You have our backing in whatever you do, one hundred percent."

Jane regarded them dubiously. She *had* asked for their advice. But what exactly was she going to say to Luke? "Maybe after the kids are asleep."

"Go now or you'll chicken out," Renée commanded.

"But the girls…"

"I'll take the baby to my house," Brooke volunteered. "She and Marly will have a ball."

Renée jumped right in. "What are friends for if not to babysit? I can style Zoey's hair. She'll love it."

"You're right." Jane got to her feet. If she didn't say something to Luke now, she might lose her chance. "Let's do it."

She stuck her feet in her pumps, grabbed her purse while Brooke scooped up Marly, and led her friends out the door.

Chapter Fourteen

After work on Wednesday, Luke was pleased to learn from Maryam that Zoey had shown no further signs of aggression toward the baby. "They were both on the quiet side today," she told him.

"Good." He'd scheduled the first available appointment—next week—for himself and Zoey with a highly recommended family counselor. Still, that marked only a first step toward helping his daughter adjust.

He also had a meeting with the attorney on Monday, which he wasn't looking forward to. The whole process dismayed him, especially since he had such profoundly mixed feelings about parting with Tina. But he had to make sure, before he talked to Ms. Lincoln, that he knew what his legal rights were.

After a light supper, he put on a kiddy exercise DVD and rolled around on the floor with the girls. Tina giggled and Zoey laughed right back, taking care not to be rough with the baby. Still, after that incident with the scissors, Luke didn't dare let down his guard.

The DVD had just ended when from outside came the tap of footsteps and the murmur of female voices. "It's Jane!" Zoey cried and ran to the door.

What a varied group of friends, Luke mused as he regarded the trio on his doorstep. Earth-mother Brooke; tall, willowy Renée; and Jane, the most beautiful of the three, with fire snapping from her eyes.

He hadn't missed her furious expression when he broke the news earlier today of seeing a lawyer about Tina. But surely Jane didn't think that bringing reinforcements would change his decision.

"Renée's offered to style Zoey's hair," she announced without preamble. "So you and I can talk."

Zoey jumped up and down. "Yay! Can we start now?"

"You bet, sweetie," the hairdresser said.

"Is it okay, Daddy?"

Luke nodded warily. At least he'd have a chance to explain about the scissors incident.

"I can take Tina with me, if that's all right. She'll enjoy Marlene's play mats," Brooke said.

"Thanks, both of you." To Zoey, Luke added, "We can delay bedtime *if* we skip reading a book tonight."

"Okay!"

She ran to put on her shoes and, within minutes, the girls were whisked away. "Thanks for arranging this." Luke gestured toward a chair, but Jane remained standing.

"About Tina," she began.

"It's for her own safety," Luke said, and described the incident at Maryam's. "I've set up a counseling appointment, but I'm afraid to delay much longer. Tina has a right to a secure home."

"I won't argue about that." Jane relaxed enough to sit down. "But there's no need to go parent-hunting. Let me adopt her."

He should have seen that coming, Luke reflected as he settled on the couch. "I'll give it some thought."

"I deserve more than 'some thought.'" Jane pressed. "I'm great with Tina, and she can grow up in this neighborhood, surrounded by friends and caring neighbors. Plus, while you're here, you can see her as often as you like."

It *would* be a simple solution. No searching for the perfect couple. No background checks or tough choices.

But now that he'd reached this point, Luke refused to take the easy way out. Even at the risk of hurting someone he cared about deeply.

"Jane, first, there's the fact that you work the same kind of long hours that I do." When she started to protest, Luke raised his hand to halt her. "Second, I have a chance to find an ideal situation for Tina, and to me that means two parents. You grew up with a largely absentee dad. Can you honestly say that's the best thing for her?"

She drummed her fingers on the arm of the chair. "Let me be sure I'm clear about this. You prefer to place Tina with a stable married couple, right?"

That summed it up. "I'd prefer to keep her myself, but since I can't, yes."

"But other than that, you think I'd make a great mom for her."

"Well, of course."

"Good." She shot to her feet as if overcome by restlessness. "Bart Ryan asked me to marry him and I'm going to accept. He's as fond of Tina as I am."

"What?" Luke didn't believe this. Jane didn't love Bart; she wasn't the sort of woman to sleep with one man when she was involved with another. "You can't marry him just to adopt a child."

"You're the one who pointed out he has feelings for me. He may be shy, but…"

"What about *your* feelings for him?" Standing up, Luke faced her sternly. "I haven't even seen you two out on a date, and I can't imagine you've had—what we shared." His voice trailed off.

"That's irrelevant," she snapped.

"A marriage of convenience isn't stable. It's absurd."

"You're hardly a good judge of what makes a stable marriage!"

He scowled. "That's a low blow."

Jane bit back whatever she'd been about to say. "You're right. I apologize. But seriously, Luke, I'm not like you. My career isn't enough to make me happy. I want more."

"And that means marrying some guy who helps you haul compost?" He might be landing a low blow himself, Luke conceded, but he had to prevent this travesty. "You're letting your maternal instincts warp your good sense."

To his dismay, tears dimmed her brown eyes. "I can't force you to give me custody. But I will marry Bart, and we'll have children, regardless of your lousy opinion of us."

"That's the last thing I have." He reached to gather Jane into a hug. More than anything, he yearned to have her relax against him and forget this nonsense. "Don't do this. Don't throw everything away."

She drew back from him. "Throw what away? Believe it or not, Luke, I have dreams that don't revolve around *you*." She turned and marched to the door. He felt too angry and confused to go after her. What the hell just happened?

He'd told her not to marry a man she obviously didn't love. Why did she refuse to listen?

And why couldn't he bear the thought that she intended to go ahead with this stupid plan anyway?

JANE STOMPED into the house and nearly tripped over Stopgap. The spaniel peered at her sorrowfully.

"I don't mean to take this out on you, but jeez!" She grabbed the wine bottle and glasses her friends had left in the living room and carried them into the kitchen. "That man's as wrapped up in himself as a...as a fried taco."

Okay, that sounded ridiculous. Still...

"I've never asked him for anything. Not once in all these years. But the one time I do, he treats me like an irresponsible idiot." Jane plunked the glasses in the sink, thrust the wine into the fridge and yanked open the freezer to reveal the remaining half gallon of praline pecan. Thanks to Luke, she was going to gain fifty pounds. She'd look like a beached whale waddling to the altar in her tentlike wedding gown, and it would be entirely his fault.

"All right, that *was* a childish thought." She stuck a spoon into the carton. "See what that man has reduced me to?"

The dog whined. In sympathy, Jane presumed.

Her wedding gown. The prospect sobered her.

Was she really going to pick out the dress of her dreams for a man who didn't keep her awake at night shivering with excitement? How could she find joy in planning the most important day of her life for a man she merely liked?

Jane dropped into a chair. She visualized Bart's craggy face, but only for an instant before she saw Luke again, violet-gray eyes shining. There was a man that a woman could love with all her heart.

If she didn't kill him first.

As for Bart, he deserved a woman who raved about *his* terrific qualities, not someone who announced their engagement to another man before she'd even said "yes" to him.

Jane jabbed the spoon repeatedly into the ice cream until she realized she was mutilating it. Disgusted, she stuck the carton back in the freezer.

She couldn't reach any conclusions tonight. Not while she was still seething.

ALTHOUGH OTHER STAFF MEMBERS went about their tasks with their normal briskness on Thursday, to Luke a dark cloud hung over the medical office. Whenever Jane spotted him, her mouth formed a hard, thin line, and her manner became coldly professional.

He'd have liked to smooth things over, but he refused to let her and Bart adopt Tina when their marriage seemed like a sham. Plus, he was irked at her for his own sake.

Becoming lovers again had meant a lot to Luke. Then, for the second time, she'd backed off in a big hurry.

He could understand her reluctance in medical school, when both of them faced difficult decisions about their careers. And he had to admit he'd been emotionally unreliable back then.

This time, though, he'd made it clear he wanted to stay involved. Surely they could work out the logistics, regardless of where he ended up. Why was she being so stubborn?

He had to put the subject aside for now, Luke reflected, and concentrate on his next patient. Valerie Nuncio was twenty-nine and had had a normal checkup only a few months earlier. However, due to a family history of breast and ovarian cancer, she'd recently had tests and was discovered to have a gene mutation that predisposed her to those diseases.

He entered the consulting room and shook hands with the dark-haired young woman in a peach-colored dress. Since she didn't require an exam, Pam hadn't asked her to undress. "Hi. I'm Dr. Van Dam."

"I'm Val." She had a firm grip. "I'd like some honest answers, Doctor."

"That's what I'm here for." He took a chair beside hers. "You're concerned about your cancer risk."

"I'm more than concerned. My sister's battling ovarian cancer and she's only thirty-five," Val told him. "I want a hysterectomy."

Luke glanced at her chart. "You haven't had children. Would you like to?"

Tears filled her eyes. "Yes, but I'm not even married yet. I can't run the risk that I'll wait too long."

"Prophylactic hysterectomies—solely for preventive purposes—aren't recommended for women under forty who might want children." Even as he spoke, Luke recognized how frightening her situation must be.

"What *is* my risk?" Val demanded.

He wished he had a conclusive answer. "It depends on a number of factors." Earlier that morning, when he'd learned from Pam that the patient had tested positive for the gene, he'd done some research and run off the results. Now he reviewed statistics and recent studies with her.

"Using oral contraceptives seems to lower the risk of ovarian cancer, but it may increase the danger of breast cancer," he told her as they went through the reports.

"Isn't ovarian cancer worse?" she asked. "It seems like you hear a lot about breast-cancer survivors, but not ovarian."

That was true. "It's harder to diagnose because the ovaries lie deep within the body," Luke explained. "As a result, it's often quite advanced by the time it's detected. The overall survival rate is between thirty-five and fifty percent."

"For my sister, it could be zero percent," she proclaimed. "If I have my ovaries removed, won't that solve the problem? I want to get on with my life."

He consulted the research. "You'd have a substantial risk reduction for both types of cancer. But at your age…"

"My sister's not that much older," she said.

What a terrible dilemma. Also, major surgery simply to prevent a disease might not be covered by her insurance, Luke pointed out.

"I need to find that out," Val agreed.

"I'd like you to undergo some counseling, too. You must be sure you've come to terms with all the issues." He wrote a prescription, since some insurance policies might cover the counseling. "Please don't rush into this decision when you're so understandably upset about your sister."

Val clutched the piece of paper. "If there were better treatments for ovarian cancer, maybe I'd run that risk. But right now, it's not worth it."

"After you've seen a counselor, let me know what you decide," Luke told her.

"You'll do it?" She regarded him questioningly. "One of the patients I met at the cancer center asked her doctor ten years ago and he refused. Now she's dying, too."

"Doctors go into medicine to heal, not to operate on the healthy," he told her. "But in the end, it's your body and your risk. Once I'm sure you've examined all the angles, I'll comply with your wishes. Meanwhile, is your sister enrolled in a clinical trial?"

She shook her head.

"Let me look into what's available to see if there's anything that might benefit her."

Val gave him a tremulous smile. "Thank you, Dr. Van Dam."

This, Luke reflected as he said goodbye, was why he yearned to get into research. Much as he enjoyed treating individuals, he wanted to do more.

As soon as he got a break, he put in a call to an old friend, Dr. Julius LaRouche. A former tennis partner of his, the cancer specialist had moved to Tennessee, where he was involved in research at Vanderbilt Medical Center.

After they caught up, Luke explained about his patient's sister and asked if Julius had come across any relevant new trials.

"As a matter of fact, yes." The man's slightly nasal voice moved along at as fast a pace as his brilliant mind. "We're testing a radical new procedure right here. You've heard of nanobots." The microscopic devices could be propelled through the bloodstream.

"Sure."

According to Julius, researchers had developed a

way to steer nanobots using resonance imaging to carry cancer-killing drugs directly to tumors. Because no new drugs were involved, the procedure didn't have to wait for lengthy government approvals.

"It's too soon to issue a report, but we're already seeing some exciting results." He paused. "Say, there's a position opening up here. We could use an OB with your clinical experience. How about putting in an application? I'll give you my recommendation."

The offer caught Luke by surprise. "I made a one-year commitment to stay here," he said. *And Nashville's almost two thousand miles away.*

"Well, I'm not sure how soon it will be filled, so keep it in mind."

"I'll do that. Thanks, Julius." Luke returned to his original purpose. "Any room in your testing for one more patient?"

"Sorry, we're full for this round."

"Are there any similar trials in Southern California?" His patient had mentioned that her sister lived nearby.

"Not that I know of," Julius said. "I wish there were. The more centers trying this technique, the better we can evaluate it."

They signed off. Well, that had been a significant but ultimately unsatisfying conversation, Luke reflected.

Something Julius had said nagged at him. Before he could pinpoint it, Pam peered in, her expression tense. "The day care is trying to reach you."

Anxiously, Luke pressed Maryam's number and prayed that everyone was safe.

"Thanks for calling back." The day-care provider sounded strained. "I thought you'd want to know that

Zoey's very upset. She's been crying, and when I asked why, she said nobody wants her."

"What?" He couldn't imagine what would give his daughter that idea. "Was there a problem at school?"

"She was fine when I met the bus," the sitter said. "I've been trying to piece together what happened since then. The children were playing in the yard and I saw her talking to the gardener working next door. Do you know Bart Ryan?"

Rage swept over Luke. If that man had done anything to hurt his child… "Yes."

"I saw him chatting with Zoey through the fence. She came running over, asking about you giving away the baby. What's going on?"

A cold chill replaced Luke's anger. He hadn't exactly made a secret of his intentions to find a new home for Tina, nor had he objected to Jane discussing the topic with Bart. Never having lived in such a small community before, he hadn't considered that his daughter might hear about this from a third party.

He explained the situation to Maryam. "It's for Tina's safety, and so I can give Zoey the attention she needs. I don't understand why she'd feel like nobody wants *her*."

"Didn't you say you were going to see Cynthia?" Maryam probed. "The sooner the better." Dr. Cynthia Lieberman, the counselor with whom he'd made an appointment, lived in Harmony Circle and had been recommended by several people, including Maryam.

"Agreed." He put in a quick call and, stressing the urgency of the situation, asked for a crisis consultation ahead of schedule. The receptionist checked with her boss and returned to say that the counselor would stay late. He could bring his daughter in at six o'clock.

"We'll be there," Luke replied. "Thank you very much."

He got back on the phone and arranged for Maryam to keep Tina late. After hanging up, he suddenly remembered that this was his on-call night. What if he was needed at the hospital?

Frustrated by this latest complication, Luke put his head down on his desk. He knew he could cope—he just needed a minute. Oh, bloody hell.

He sensed Jane's reassuring presence even before he lifted his head. "Pam mentioned a problem with the kids," she said from the doorway. "Do you need me to cover for you tonight?"

To Luke, she seemed bathed in an angelic glow. "I don't deserve it, but yes. I'll cover for you next week."

"Don't worry about it," she said. "Are the girls okay?"

"Basically, yes." He didn't want to mention Bart's role in what had happened. After all, this wasn't really the gardener's fault. "I'm sorry for what I said about your maternal instincts warping your judgment. You have incredible maternal instincts *and* great judgment."

She could have seized the opportunity to drive home her point about adopting Tina. To Luke's relief, she took the high road. "We'll discuss this when you aren't so stressed."

"Yes. Good." Maybe he should reconsider insisting on a two-parent home. Maybe he should reconsider everything, Luke thought as she left.

He couldn't let her marry Bart. He didn't know what he had to offer instead, but his gut had clenched when Julius suggested moving to Nashville. Something held him here—and yet something also held him back from Jane. What the hell could it be?

For now, he had to focus on his daughter. As for whatever lay buried inside him, maybe Dr. Lieberman could help him sort that out, as well.

Chapter Fifteen

Jane's anger at Luke had vanished the moment she saw him with his head on his desk. And not only because she shared his concern for the kids.

Last night, he'd haunted her dreams. There'd been a scene where Luke was in bed with her, whispering words she couldn't quite understand, and then he'd been beckoning her from down a hallway. When she approached, he always seemed to be fading around the next corner.

Deciphering that dream didn't require an expert. Against her better judgment, she'd been seduced by the man in medical school but managed to convince herself she'd get over him. Now she'd fallen for him again, and this time her feelings resonated much more deeply.

Jane didn't see how she was going to recover. But she'd find a way.

When her four-thirty appointment canceled, Jane drove home early and went out into the garden. Last weekend, she'd bought tomato, eggplant, parsley and basil plants and set them in place in her garden ready for planting. Nearby patches of bare soil bore markers to show where she'd sown seeds for lettuce and onions and, in a separate area to accommodate their future sprawl, zucchini.

If she married Bart, they'd spend hours gardening. Together, they'd whip up healthy meals and, afterward, they'd relax side by side to read or watch a documentary on TV. Until they had kids, although no doubt they'd eventually incorporate the little ones into their routine.

She doubted they'd ever quarrel. Living with Bart would be practically as peaceful as living by herself. And just as dull. How unfair that she'd kept him hanging for days, when her answer had to be no.

Still, Jane hesitated, trying to figure out what to say. She'd never been in a position to break someone's heart before. Had their situations been reversed, though, she'd prefer the plain truth, wouldn't she?

Her side gate swung open. Since hardly anyone ventured into her backyard unannounced, Jane turned in surprise.

Bart must have heard her thinking about him, or else their minds had fallen into the same track, because here he was. Mellow light played over his familiar lean figure dressed in jeans and T-shirt, with an Angels baseball cap atop his shaggy hair.

He stood sideways as if preparing for a rapid getaway. Always before, he'd ambled in here without a care in the world.

Jane hurried over. "It's good to see you. Listen, Bart, I meant to get back to you sooner…"

"You're not mad?" he asked.

"About what?"

"What I said to Zoey."

That stumped her. "I didn't know you said anything to Zoey."

He flushed. "I shot my big mouth off. Told her we wanted to adopt the baby. She looked like I'd slapped her."

"Oh, my gosh." *That* explained the crisis this afternoon. Apparently Luke hadn't mentioned his plans to his daughter.

"Never occurred to me she didn't know all about it. I figured she'd be pleased." He dragged off the cap and twisted it in his hands. "Jane, I never meant to upset the little girl."

"Luke's taking her to a counselor." Jane had confidence in Cynthia's ability to help them through this difficulty.

"I really mucked things up." Bart grimaced.

"Counseling's a good idea in any event, what with her mother remarrying," Jane told him. "It isn't your fault she didn't know. Luke may have been trying to protect her, but secrets have a way of getting out."

"They sure do, thanks to me." He appeared determined to punish himself.

"I'm the one who told you about Tina. I should have cleared that with Luke first."

They both fell silent. Studying Bart, Jane reflected how much she cared about him. But not enough to sustain a marriage. Much as she hated to admit it, Luke had been right. *You can't marry a man you don't love.*

That, she supposed, was how Luke must feel about her. Fond and admiring, but nothing more. Pain wrenched inside her at the thought.

From Brooke and Oliver's yard next door drifted the scent of grilling steaks, a reminder of how easily this conversation might be overheard. "Please, come inside so we can talk."

"I'm more at home outdoors." Bart gave the cap another twist. "I've been doing some soul-searching this afternoon."

"Yes?"

"About you and me." He paused.

It hit Jane that she wasn't the only person with doubts. The uncharacteristic wavering of Bart's gaze bolstered her suspicion. "You're rethinking your proposal?"

"That's a terrible thing for a man to do." He cleared his throat. "Jane, you're an amazing woman. The thing is, I'd be doing you a disservice. All this emotional turmoil doesn't suit me. What kind of husband would I make? I thought you and I could have a happy, peaceful marriage, but that's not realistic. People have feelings, and they fight and hurt each other. I'm not sure I'm up to it."

It struck her that, during Bart's proposal, he hadn't once mentioned love. "You implied that you'd been in love once," she said. "Is that right?"

His head bobbed in the affirmative.

"How did you feel about that other woman? Was it the same as with me?" She wasn't sure what spurred her to ask. Call it a hunch.

"No," Bart conceded. "I was younger. I had wild, crazy feelings for her. Maybe it was too strong, the kind of thing that's meant to burn out. I was afraid we'd drive each other over the edge."

"I think that's an edge people ought to go over once in a lifetime." Jane shuddered at the image. "I'm not sure why I said that. I'm hardly the leap-off-a-cliff type, am I?"

"You're honest and real," Bart told her. "That's why you're so great. Can we still be friends, Jane?"

"Absolutely."

He didn't stick around as he normally would to look over her plantings. Instead, with a relieved nod, he scurried through the gate.

How ironic that she was stuck with those wild, crazy feelings for Luke, Jane reflected as she went into the house. Now she had to figure out how to get rid of them.

And move on with the business of establishing a family.

LUKE PARKED in front of the Fullerton office building that housed Dr. Lieberman's office. Most of the parking spaces sat empty at this hour.

"Why do I have to see a doctor?" Zoey demanded from the passenger seat. "I'm not sick."

While Luke had explained the situation several times, either his daughter hadn't understood or was seeking reassurance. A thin red rim around her eyes testified to her distress.

"She's a special kind of doctor who helps heal people's feelings when they get hurt," he said.

"Did I hurt your feelings?" she asked as she got out.

Luke locked the car behind them. "No, sweetie, I hurt yours. I didn't mean to keep secrets from you. Daddies make mistakes, too."

On the elevator ride to the third floor, Zoey chewed her lip. "Does she give shots?"

Luke took her hand. "No. She's the kind of doctor who talks to you."

"Oh, like a *shrink*."

"Where'd you hear that term?" he asked in surprise.

"In a cartoon." She squared her shoulders. "I guess this won't be too bad."

In the counselor's reception area, the front desk stood empty. Her secretary must have left for the day.

A woman in her fifties, her gray-streaked hair worn in a neat pageboy, was sorting through mail at a side table. She set the envelopes down when she spotted them. "You must be Dr. Van Dam and Zoey. I'm Dr. Lieberman. Call me Cynthia." She extended her hand.

"I'm Luke." As he greeted the woman her warmth and confident manner put him at ease. He also liked the way she shook hands with Zoey, treating the child as an equal.

In her private office, bright colors enlivened the walls, while children's books and toys lay scattered on low tables. Cynthia gestured them into the comfortable chairs. "I'd like to talk to you both for a few minutes, and then to Zoey alone. Is that all right?" She spoke directly to the girl.

Hesitantly, Zoey agreed.

In response to Cynthia's questioning, Luke sketched the situation with his ex-wife and Tina, and his decision to find a new home for the baby in order to focus on Zoey. "I should have told her about this sooner. I'm sorry she heard it from a stranger."

"Bart isn't a stranger," Zoey corrected. "He's Jane's friend."

The therapist smiled. "You can tell me all about Bart and Jane and Tina in a minute, okay?" With that, she asked Luke to step into the waiting room.

"Of course." He went out, and, although he wished he'd brought medical journals to read, the parenting magazine he picked up proved interesting. "Protecting

Your Child Online." There was a topic he ought to learn more about. "Peer Pressure and Your Pre-Adolescent Daughter." Definitely worthwhile. Luke pocketed a subscription card.

He was absorbed in an article about teaching children to manage their finances when the inner door opened. A glance at his watch revealed that half an hour had passed.

Zoey blew her nose on a tissue, then straightened. "Hi, Daddy."

"You okay, sweetheart?" He held his arms out for a hug. She clung to him. "I like Cynthia."

"Thank you," said the psychologist, observing them from her consulting room. "I like you, too."

Zoey gazed at Luke earnestly. "Daddy, I'm sorry I cut up Tina's bunny. Can I buy her a new one with my allowance?"

"You bet." Luke hadn't mentioned the incident to Cynthia. "You told the doctor about that?"

"I was mean to Tina. I wished Grandma gave me the bunny. That bracelet itches my arm." She blinked away a tear. "I love Tina. I don't want her to go away."

His throat tightened. "I don't want her to, either."

Cynthia opened a large plastic bin of toys. "Zoey, is it okay if I tell your father the other things we discussed while you play out here?"

His daughter nodded.

"Will you be okay by yourself for a few minutes? If you get worried, feel free to join us." Cynthia watched the girl's expression closely.

"I'm fine." Zoey plucked a puzzle from the box.

Luke accompanied Cynthia into her cheerful office. "I should redo my examining rooms like this," he joked.

She indicated a mural of Alice in Wonderland. "I'm not sure most women would care to have the Mad Hatter watch their yearly exam."

"You're right." Relaxing, he took a seat. "Does Zoey think I was angry about her cutting up the bunny?"

"She does."

"I understand that she might expect punishment. But why would she think I don't want her?"

Cynthia pressed her fingertips together. "She's already been bounced around between her mother and grandmother. When she heard that you were finding a new home for the baby, she figured you might give her up, too."

No wonder his daughter had been crying. "Nothing could be further from my mind. I was trying to ensure Zoey gets the attention she deserves."

"Children don't think the way adults do," the counselor noted. "Since they believe they're the center of the universe, they feel overly responsible for others' reactions."

Luke shuddered at his mistake. "I love both girls. Obviously, I've had far more time to become attached to Zoey. Since Tina's only been with us for two weeks, I imagined I'd be doing her a favor finding her a two-parent family."

"I can't make that decision for you." Cynthia glanced at her notepad as if to refresh her memory. "But you have a stronger bond with the baby than you realize. From what you've told me, her mother regarded you as her own surrogate father, and you've known Tina literally since she was born. As she grows, those connections should help give her a sense of belonging."

He'd never thought of it that way. "I've been tearing

myself apart over giving her up. I'm glad I won't have to." A burden lifted from his spirit as he spoke. "I hope Zoey will be reassured when she learns Tina's staying with us."

"I believe so. As for Zoey's mother, Zoey has a lot of abandonment issues to deal with, but fundamentally, she's got both feet on the ground. She opened up and talked freely, which shows that she trusts adults. You and her mother can take credit for that." The counselor regarded him thoughtfully. "Do you have any other questions or concerns?"

"I suppose I have a few abandonment issues of my own," Luke conceded. "My mom left when I was young. I can't help wondering how that affects my abilities as a parent."

"You strike me as a loving and stable father who has a strong tie to his daughter," Cynthia said. "I suggest a few more sessions to sort things out during this transitional stage in all your lives, and I'd be happy to talk further about your childhood experiences. We could start that process now, if you like."

He decided against it. "Zoey's waiting. And there's no rush."

They arose. "I understand you live around the corner from me. I'm glad to have you as a neighbor," the counselor said.

Luke shook her hand. "I'll call your office tomorrow for our next appointment."

He collected his daughter, who returned the toys to their box without protest and happily took his hand. How had he missed what now seemed obvious clues about Zoey's emotions? He'd been totally wrong about her feelings toward Tina, for instance.

As they got in the car, Zoey said, "Cynthia's a good doctor."

"The best," Luke concurred. "Don't worry about Tina. She's going to stay with us and be your sister always. I hope you feel better."

She paused as if taking her internal temperature. "A bit."

"What else is wrong?"

Her lips pressed together. "Why doesn't Mommy come see me?" she asked at last.

"She will," Luke said. "When her schedule settles down."

"I guess." Zoey stuck her hands in her pockets.

"My mom left when I was four years old," he reminded her. "But we stayed in touch. That's your Grandma Marie.

"I have another grandma?" she asked.

Stunned, he said, "You've met Grandma Marie." The last time had been—what?—two years ago. "Remember when we flew to San Francisco?"

"Oh, yeah. She makes those paintings." She frowned. "They're kinda sad."

"I think so, too."

The fact that Zoey had nearly forgotten Luke's mother wasn't surprising, he supposed. She rarely remembered to send birthday or Christmas presents, let alone visit.

Marie Van Dam had gotten fed up with being a mother by the time Luke came along. *Guess it's like Kris said. I was one child too many.*

He recalled a bitter argument he'd had as a teenager, when his brother had shouted, "Mom never would have left if it weren't for you."

For some odd reason, Luke had secretly agreed with him. But why?

He caught the edge of an even older memory. Angry words. A terrible fear that sent darkness spiraling through him. Good Lord, how long had he been repressing *that?*

As Cynthia had said, children often took too much responsibility for adults' behavior. Maybe it was time Luke confronted the subject straight on, and not just by talking to a counselor.

He set the issue aside to spend the next few hours concentrating on the girls. And enjoyed a sweet moment when Zoey helped him put her sister to bed. "I'll buy you a new bunny," she announced from beside the crib. "You're staying with us forever."

"That's a promise," Luke seconded.

Once he'd tucked Zoey into bed, he settled in the living room and took out his phone. Time to face something he'd buried long ago and that had been ticking away like a time bomb ever since.

No matter how much the truth hurt, he'd rather deal with it than keep on wondering.

Chapter Sixteen

After dinner on Thursday, Jane finally tried something she'd been considering for a long time. She checked out an online dating Web site a friend had recommended.

Mr. Right had to be out there, and finding him was a matter of logistics. Before Luke arrived, she'd exhausted her pool of friends of friends, and working in an office with mostly women provided few chances to encounter men. She was ready to take the plunge.

The site let her input her zip code, which allayed her doubts about meeting someone who lived nearby. As for her profile, Jane had heard never to put in identifiable personal data, and her friend had advised not to say she was a doctor, because that might attract gold diggers. Instead, she indicated she worked in the medical profession, and listed her interests and preferences.

Now, what kind of man was she seeking?

Mid-thirties. Tall enough to gaze down at me hungrily. Gray eyes that turn purple when he's passionate. Thick brown hair that flops in his eyes when he forgets to cut it. A slightly crooked nose from a football injury, and a cleft in his left cheek.

Oh, honestly, *that* was never going to fly.

Propping her elbows on the desk, Jane rested her face in her hands. Okay, so she craved Luke, but he was unavailable in every sense. Absorbed in his work, averse to long-term commitments, emotionally remote. A lot like her dad.

The other guys who'd shown an interest in her over the years hadn't excited her the way he did, but, she reminded herself, it was all a numbers game. Meet enough men and she *would* find someone with the right qualities.

On the screen, she filled out a few more specifics and turned her future over to the computer program. *Make me a match.* Or a few hundred. She'd winnow them out.

Her phone rang. Not surprising, since she was on call, and sure enough, the hospital needed her. Another miracle was on the way.

More than one miracle, Jane hoped as she hurried to her car. There might be magic on the Internet, if she searched long enough.

MARIE VAN DAM ANSWERED the phone sounding distracted, as if she'd been dragged away from something important. Come to think of it, she usually gave that impression, Luke reflected.

Her tone softened slightly when she heard his greeting. "How's it going?"

"Pauline got married again. I took Zoey to a counselor today to help her deal with it." He decided to get straight to the point. "That started me thinking about you. I mean, about when you left us."

Luke's mother released a long breath. "I figured we'd have this conversation eventually."

"Which conversation?" he asked.

"The one about how your awful mother abandoned her children," Marie said with a cynical edge.

He didn't like the way she dismissed his attempt to heal old wounds. "I'm not trying to beat you up emotionally," Luke replied stiffly. "It's that I'm having trouble understanding some stuff." Might as well blurt the whole thing. "Was I the reason you left?"

His mother made a choking noise. "What on earth gave you that idea?"

"Kris blames me." Although he and his brother had more or less moved past their teenage quarrel, they'd never become close. "The truth is, I've always figured I was responsible, too."

"Don't be ridiculous." As usual, Marie sidestepped any venture into emotional territory. "If it helps, I apologize, okay? I hope you're satisfied. Now let's leave it at that."

I hope you're satisfied. The words he'd heard her say years before. He'd been very small, quaking as his mother's voice exploded at his father in the next room: *You pushed me to have another baby. I hope you're satisfied! I warned you I couldn't handle this.* Along with the memory came a stab of primal fear, not the rational anxiety of an adult but the terror of a four-year-old on the brink of losing the most important person in his world.

"You argued with Dad," Luke recalled. "Kris and I were listening. You said it was Dad's idea to have another baby, and you couldn't handle it."

Silence descended on the other end of the line. He half expected his mother to once again brush off his concerns.

"You boys heard that?" she said instead. "I thought you were asleep."

"Kris never forgave me for driving you away. We fought about it later," he admitted.

"Oh, Lord. I never dreamed that you knew." She halted, breathing hard.

Never having had such an open discussion with his mother before, Luke wasn't sure what to say. He simply waited.

Marie cleared her throat. "I realized after Quent's birth that I wasn't ready to have children, but I tried to make the best of it. Then Kris came along, and instead of pitching in as he'd promised, your dad spent more time at work. I moved back with my parents for a while, but he begged me to return and try for a girl. My parents played a guilt trip on me, so I did."

"Instead you got me," Luke muttered. "Another boy."

"You were a sweet little kid who never gave me any trouble," his mother responded. "But your father paid even less attention to his family than before. I got so mad, I screamed at everybody, including you kids. I imagined that if I left again, your father might come to his senses and maybe we'd work something out. Instead, he refused to bend an inch and treated me like the enemy. Finally I said the hell with it."

"I thought you went to find yourself."

"Well, that, too," she admitted.

"Didn't you miss us?" Luke disliked the quaver in his voice. Couldn't help it, though.

"Very much. I cried a lot," she admitted. "But San Francisco was an exciting place to be thirty years ago—it still is—and I got busy making up for lost time. I was only eighteen when I got married. Remember your dad's ten years older than me. This was my first taste of independence."

She'd been the same age as Annie when she became a mother. Luke had always pictured his parents as mature and settled.

"I know I let you kids down," she went on. "And I'm sorry you felt responsible for my leaving. But my life suits me. I can't live it to please someone else."

"No one expects you to." Luke wasn't sure what he'd hoped for. A more profound reconciliation, perhaps. Still, at least now he understood what had happened.

"And, Luke?" Marie said.

"Yes?"

"It's okay that you don't like my paintings."

They both chuckled. Obviously he hadn't hidden his reaction as well as he'd thought. "I love you, Mom."

"I love you, too. I'm sorry I couldn't show it more." That was clearly the best she could offer.

After hanging up, Luke found Kris's number and called his brother. They had a lot to talk about, too.

ON FRIDAY, Jane droved into her parking space behind the office as Luke was emerging from his car. He waited for her, a trench coat emphasizing the strong lines of his body.

"Thanks for subbing for me last night," he said. "I owe you. Busy?"

"Only one delivery, and at a very reasonable hour."

A darling little boy with thick dark hair and beautiful chocolate skin. "How'd it go with Cynthia Lieberman?" They'd both arrived early, so there was no rush to get into the office.

"I learned a lot."

"About what?"

"I completely misjudged the situation with Zoey," Luke conceded. "And I've decided to keep Tina."

Jane felt a tug of disappointment. Still, she hadn't really expected him to let her have the baby, and besides, they'd be right next door, at least for a while. "You know I'll help as much as I can, as long as you're in the neighborhood."

"You aren't upset?"

"I'm glad for you and the girls," she told him truthfully.

He still made no move to go inside. "I'd like you to know I'm making a fresh start."

"You already did that," she pointed out. "You moved to Brea less than six weeks ago."

"I meant in the way I look at things."

Standing this close, his body heat sheltered her from the early-morning chill. As he leaned toward her, Jane felt a keen awareness of his mouth, and how much she ached to kiss it.

You are not going to do this, McKay. She took a step back. "Well, good for you."

"Aren't you going to ask what I mean?"

"I've got a lot on my mind." *Like putting you in the past.* "Save it for another day."

He released a long breath. "Okay, no personal stuff. But you might be interested to hear about my idea for what we could do with that MRI scanner."

She didn't give a rat's nest about the MRI. "You should discuss that with Wendy Clark."

"Jane!" Luke burst out. "If we can do research right here, it means I won't have to leave."

"That'll be wonderful for your patients." Did he expect her to leap for joy like some lovestruck intern? She wasn't even sure she *wanted* him to stick around. It made her even more determined to find the right guy.

"Is this about Bart?" he asked.

"Bart?"

"The man you might or might not marry. You aren't really going through with that, are you?" he demanded.

"Our plans have changed." Might as well come clean. "We decided we didn't really suit."

To her indignation, Luke grinned. "A wise choice."

His smugness stretched her patience to the breaking point. "Yes. It frees me to make a fresh start, too," she snapped.

"Jane, what's this about?" The way Luke kept verbally poking at her made Jane even angrier.

"Last night I posted my profile on a dating Web site. When I checked this morning, there were five responses."

"You did what?" He caught her arm.

She shrugged free. "Bart wasn't the right guy. But I'm going to find him."

What a bunch of nonsense and colored smoke. The man she yearned to spend her life with stood right here, staring at her with a dumbstruck expression. But while the business about a fresh start and sticking around might sound enticing, all it meant was that he'd go on being the boy next door who expected them to be friends with privileges.

"I'm sure we've both got plenty to do," Jane concluded, and sailed inside.

At the nurses' station, Rosemary Tran glanced past Jane's shoulder. "What's wrong with Dr. Van Dam? He looks as if someone just slapped him."

"Someone ought to," Jane said, and walked on.

ALL DAY, LUKE TRIED to figure out what was going on with Jane. She seemed mad at him. Was this because of Tina? Yet she'd claimed to support his decision.

As for the Internet business, it made no sense. She had a man, right here. They'd shared so much, and now Luke might not be leaving after all. Sure, there'd be issues to work out after Sean's return, but with a full patient list, the practice could easily accommodate a third doctor.

The possibility that Jane was shedding him as easily as Bart ate away at Luke. That didn't seem like the Jane he knew. If he confronted her now, though, he had no idea what he'd say. Besides, she'd turned prickly as a pincushion.

After work, he collected his daughters from Maryam's. "Let's go shopping. I want to buy Tina a bunny, remember?" Zoey said when they reached home.

"Later this evening." He had a list of groceries to get, as well.

"What's for dinner?" His daughter prowled into the kitchen. "Tina likes macaroni and cheese."

"She's too young for that." As a six-month-old, the baby was still on formula augmented by baby food and mashed fruit. "Are you hinting that *you'd* like macaroni and cheese?"

"Yeah."

"Let's fix it together," he suggested.

Zoey fetched a box from the pantry and Luke put water on to boil. He showed her how to measure the milk and salt, while Tina rolled around on the floor and occasionally sat up to watch.

Day by day, they were becoming a real family, he reflected as they ate companionably. If only Jane were here.

Had just a week passed since they made love? He'd been running on all cylinders, what with Pauline's marriage, Zoey's acting out, the arrest of Tina's grand-mother and his struggle to plan the baby's future. Jane should understand how complicated his life had become. Why was she shutting him out again, as she'd done ten years ago?

Luke wanted so much more from her, he couldn't believe she didn't feel the same way. For heaven's sake, they loved each other.

The lights in the room seemed to dim. He'd never thought his feelings through before, but now he recog-nized the utter truth of them.

He'd held Jane at arm's length, driving her away because of old, unrecognized fears. She'd sensed them, and she'd refused to accept anything less than full emo-tional commitment.

Now what was he going to do about it?

"Daddy!" Zoey called. "Somebody's at the door."

His spirits lifted. Then, halfway to the entrance, he heard the chatter of girlish voices. Not Jane, after all.

On the porch, Suzy Ching thrust a flyer into his hand. "You have to come to our party tomorrow afternoon, three o'clock. It's at the Lorenzes' house."

"We're celebrating Historic Harmony Circle," Carly piped up. "That's what we've called our Web pages."

"There'll be fresh-baked snacks," added Brittany.

He skimmed the colorful flyer. "I'm impressed with the way you guys put this together."

"You haven't even seen the site yet." Carly greeted Zoey with a hug. "It went live this afternoon. Can we come in and show you?"

"Sure."

The girls provided the address. On Luke's laptop, sharp graphics leaped out, proclaiming "Historic Harmony Circle" above a professional-quality layout of photos and text.

There was Minnie's cottage, sunlight gleaming on the handcrafted shutters and willow porch furniture. Beside it ran an interview in which the elderly woman recalled the World War II years before most of the development was built.

At the girls' excited urging, Luke clicked to the next page. "That's you, Daddy!" Zoey exclaimed.

Sure enough, the camera had caught him hefting a trash can filled with compost from Bart's truck, and there was Jane, dumping the contents onto her garden. Even half-covered with dirt, she looked beautiful.

"There's the pool party." Brittany directed his gaze to a montage of shots from the potluck. One showed Jane entering the enclosure, her arms encircling a bowl of pasta salad. She wore a wistful expression as she peered at someone just out of the scene.

At me.

"Look!" Zoey pointed to another photo.

Carly had captured Luke surrounded by new neighbors. Instead of paying attention to his companions, Luke's tiny image peered eagerly into the distance, his face filled with yearning.

For Jane.

His chest tightened. Why hadn't he recognized sooner how much he loved her?

This morning, she'd acted as if she'd already written him off. He had to win her back.

For his entire adult life, Luke had drawn women easily. He'd never had to break through a barrier to win a lady's heart. Now he had no idea how to proceed.

Taking the mouse, Carly clicked on a link that read "Weddings." "This is my favorite section."

"Mine, too," Suzy said.

"There's Mom," crowed Brittany as a new array of photos appeared.

On the steps of a church stood Carly and Brittany's parents, Diane and Josh Lorenz, flanked by their daughters. "We wore dark red because it was Christmas," Carly explained.

"It was cute the way Josh proposed," her stepsister volunteered. "Mom thought he was fixing up his house to sell and move away. Instead, he asked her to pick out the bedroom curtains *she* liked because he hoped we'd be moving in with him."

Lower on the page, Luke glimpsed Jane in a pink bridesmaid's dress at Brooke's wedding. To his eye, she outshone fellow bridesmaid Renée. He supposed it would be rude to consider anyone more beautiful than Brooke was in her bridal gown.

"Can you believe Oliver knelt down in the sprinklers when he proposed to Brooke?" Suzy giggled. "He was imitating her favorite romantic scene from a TV show, where it was raining."

"Since it rarely rains around here, he went with sprinklers," Carly explained to Zoey.

"Rafe and Sherry had a good story, too." Brittany indicated a picture of Luke's landlords in their wedding finery. "She'd pawned her favorite diamond earrings to pay her bills. Rafe redeemed them instead of buying a ring."

"She didn't get a ring?" Zoey asked.

"Oh, yeah," Suzy said. "He bought her one later."

"You've done an impressive job with this site," Luke told his visitors. "You could hire yourselves out as Web designers."

"Carly did most of the work," Suzy told him.

"You still have to come to our party," Brittany informed him. "There'll be raspberry chocolate cake."

"Yes!" Zoey cried. "Can we, Daddy?"

"Of course."

With only half his attention, Luke listened to the girls reviewing their plans for tomorrow. In the meantime, he began making important ones of his own.

Chapter Seventeen

If there was magic on the Internet, it eluded Jane.

She should have been more precise about age, she reflected on Saturday morning as she read through the list of responses. She'd hesitated to specify a range, in case Mr. Perfect fell just outside the parameters, but she had no interest in an arthritic seventy-two-year-old whom she suspected hoped for a nurse. Medical profession indeed.

None of the other prospects appealed to her, either. Neurotic, egotistical or just plain boring…slim pickings.

Her phone rang. She hesitated, noticing that the caller's number was blocked, but decided to take a chance. "Yes?"

"This is the answering service, Dr. McKay. You're needed at your office immediately," said a woman.

"I'm not on call."

"This is urgent. Please report to your office at once." The caller hung up.

How odd. Normally the service summoned Jane to the hospital. In fact, her office was closed on Saturdays.

Come to think of it, that woman had sounded suspiciously like Brooke. Her number should have shown on the display but perhaps Brooke was using someone else's phone.

What on earth was she up to? Perhaps a surprise. It occurred to her Sean might have come to visit unexpectedly. She checked the blog where he was recording his experiences, but found no mention of a trip home.

Perhaps she'd mistaken the voice. It could be a practical joke; over the years, many people had acquired this phone number. Perhaps she should call Brooke to double-check. Still, if her friends *were* planning a surprise, she hated to spoil it.

Jane decided to go. She didn't exactly have a busy morning ahead, anyway.

She changed from her baggy sweats to slacks and a sweater, and applied light makeup. Thanks to Renée's talents, her hair required only a quick brush to look shiny and soft.

A few minutes later, driving along Central Avenue, Jane swung by the front of the office in an effort to spot whatever was being plotted. With the shades drawn, she couldn't see inside.

What the heck. She was too curious to simply go home.

In the back, Jane found Luke's car occupying its usual space. Had the same woman summoned him, or was he involved in this?

Cautiously, she entered through the rear door into the quiet emptiness of the hallway. Her body quivered at a rush of memories from the evening when she and Luke had made love. His mouth on hers, his hands cupping her breasts…

She had to stop doing this.

"Hello?" No answer.

Jane passed the nurses' station. Above the desk, someone had hung a streamer dangling paper cutout booties and bottles. Was this a baby shower?

At a bend in the hallway, she glimpsed light streaming out of Luke's office. Teddy-bear-shaped Mylar balloons clustered around the door frame.

"Okay, this is cute," Jane called. "Whose baby are we celebrating?"

Luke ducked to avoid the balloons as he emerged. His smile seemed uncharacteristically twitchy. "Come in and I'll explain."

She got a weird feeling about this. "Please tell me this isn't what I think."

He blinked. "What's that?"

As Jane strode in, he retreated. Suspiciously, she peered around his room for an infant. Nothing, unless he'd hidden it behind the desk.

"You snared another baby, didn't you?" Jane challenged. "Let me guess. A besotted unmarried mom has bequeathed her little darling to the great Dr. Van Dam, and you plan to sweet-talk me into helping me raise it."

"Not exactly," he said.

She assumed a dignified stance, marred slightly when a low-hanging pink streamer got tangled in her hair. Jane pushed it away. "Then what?"

"You want a family, right? What would you say to two adorable little girls, and a father thrown in for good measure?" he asked.

I can't have heard right. She leaned against the desk to steady her suddenly wobbly knees. "Would you clarify, please?"

"I'm asking you to marry me, Jane." His gray eyes

shone with violet depths. "Seemed premature for wedding bells, so I figured the baby angle might be fun."

There had to be a catch. "Luke, we've known each other how long? You've never showed the least inclination to... You've never considered me your... I'm not buying this."

He had never looked more befuddled. "I mean this, Jane. Why is it so hard to believe?"

"You may have conned Brooke into calling me but I'm not that gullible." What on earth was he trying to pull?

Determination replaced his confusion. "I didn't explain very well. Why don't you sit down."

Since her legs refused to resume their normal function, she dropped into the nearest chair. "Well?"

Then Luke did something so outrageous that Jane feared she'd dreamed this entire episode. He got down on one knee in front of her.

The most elusive man she'd ever met gazed up at her pleadingly. "I've been running away from getting hurt all my life. Then I discovered that nothing could hurt worse than losing you." He swallowed hard. "I don't pretend I'll make an ideal husband. I can be clueless, as you know better than anyone. But we belong together. Marry me."

Yes. The answer stuck in Jane's throat. After holding her emotions in check for so long, she didn't trust them now. Besides, why did he imagine he was the only person who feared getting hurt?

"What I feel goes beyond love," Luke went on. "It would kill me to lose you. I breathe you, Jane. You're part of me and I want to be part of you, forever."

He fumbled in his pocket and retrieved a jeweler's box. Surely he hadn't bought a ring! Not the Luke Van

Dam who'd slept with her in medical school and then accepted their estrangement with no sign of regret.

As Jane's thoughts tumbled over each other, he pried open the box. Against black velvet sparkled a flower-shaped ring with jeweled petals.

He took a deep breath. "If you prefer a diamond, we can exchange it. Zoey insisted it was perfect, with you being a gardener and all."

"Zoey picked my ring?"

"When the girls and I went shopping for the decorations last night, we stopped at a jewelry store. I told Zoey I was buying you a ring as a present and she insisted on making the choice."

She couldn't believe this. "So your daughter knew about the proposal before I did?"

"I just said it was a gift. I don't think she understood the ramifications."

"Well, I'm sure Brooke did. Who else knows?"

"The Little Foxes helped decorate on the condition that I give them the balloons and streamers for their party this afternoon." His face flushed. "I'm not good at this stuff, Jane. I'm doing my best to be romantic."

Her fingers grazed his hand as she reached toward the ring. How real he felt.

She definitely wasn't dreaming.

Inside Jane, a swell of emotions threatened to explode. She'd fallen in love with an unattainable dream because that was what her heart needed: an impossible love, a devotion that transcended limitations. But while she was struggling to protect herself, Luke had matured into a man capable of loving her back. A man who *did* love her.

"I can't believe…" Her voice caught.

"Please," he said. "Finish that sentence."

Restraint vanished. "I love you, too, like a whirlwind and an ocean storm and a volcano erupting all in one. I love you so much my head might spin right off." Jane halted, breathing hard, as if she'd run all the way from safety to the edge of a cliff—a cliff that overlooked a glorious new vista.

"Marry me?"

"Yes!" She threw her arms around him so vigorously that they both tumbled to the floor.

On the way down, he kissed her hungrily. Lying there, Jane got lost in his strength and the wonderful sensation of his body against hers. She had no idea how much time had passed until Luke said, "Would you say yes again? I want to savor it."

"You bet," she said. "Yes, yes, yes!"

They'd have made love, she felt certain, except that far too many people knew they were here and no doubt awaited the good news. Instead, they sat up and Luke slipped the ring on her finger.

A little loose, but that was easily fixed. "Zoey has great taste, by the way."

"She'll be thrilled when she sees you wearing it."

They kissed again, and sat grinning at each other until common sense prevailed. Finally they got up, retrieved the champagne left from her birthday and took down the decorations for the Little Foxes.

Jane made a mental note to reclaim them after the party. Because in view of Luke's talent for attracting babies, she never knew when they might need them again.

MUCH AS LUKE LONGED to have Jane to himself, he knew that had to wait. So, after they drove away separately, he swung by Brooke's house. There he retrieved the girls, handed over the decorations and quietly assured Brooke that all had gone wonderfully well but that she'd have to get the details from Jane.

At home, he barely contained his excitement while fixing lunch and listening to Zoey's account of how Tina and Marlene had become best friends. She'd woven an entire fantasy about how the two babies would grow up together.

Indeed they would—right next door to each other. Just before she took off in her car, Jane had said, "You'll be moving into my house, right? Good. It's bigger, and I could use the help in the garden."

He'd laughed. "Gladly."

They'd agreed to share their news with Zoey together and attend the Little Foxes' celebration as a family. Jane would arrive at Luke's shortly before the party. First, though, she'd wanted to handle a few matters, like removing her profile from the Internet and thanking Brooke for her help.

Luke used the girls' quiet time to call his parents with the news.

"I remember Jane from when you were in med school," his father said. "Great girl. Always liked her better than Pauline."

"You were way ahead of me," Luke told him.

As for his mom, she said, "I promise not to give you a painting for a wedding present. But I would appreciate an invitation."

"Are you kidding? You and Dad are the guests of honor!"

"We haven't seen each other in over a decade. I suppose he can manage not to yell at me this once," Marie said.

"He's much mellower than he used to be." Grandparenthood had accomplished that.

"Glad to hear it." Marie wished Luke well and hung up.

He reached Kris, who congratulated Luke warmly. "You didn't mention a fiancée the other night."

"I didn't know she'd say yes."

"Well, I envy you," Kris admitted. "I've wrecked two engagements. At thirty-six, I may have to accept that there isn't a right woman for me."

"I'm only a year and half younger," Luke reminded him. "You've got time. By the way, any chance of you being my best man?"

"Anytime, any place, bro."

A short while later, their older brother, Quent, also gladly agreed to join the wedding party. "E-mail me when you set the date."

"Will do. And bring the kids," Luke told him. "I'd like my girls to get to know their cousins."

"Excellent idea."

He'd barely clicked off when Zoey peeked into the kitchen, where he'd retreated to stay as far out of earshot as possible. "Who was that on the phone?"

"Your Uncle Quent."

"Oh." She seemed disappointed. "Is it time to go to the party?"

"Almost." Out the window, he caught sight of Jane. "Look who's here."

As she came in, Luke drank in the sight of her. Had

a future bride ever looked more radiant? It wasn't just his imagination, either.

It occurred to him that he was beaming right back. And that he'd probably continue to do so for the next, oh, fifty years.

"I missed you!" Zoey cried by way of greeting. "Where's Stopgap?"

Jane chuckled. "He's staying home today. You can play with him later."

"I've hardly seen you all week. Did you and Daddy fight?" Zoey demanded as Jane entered.

"We've just been busy." She and Luke moved toward each other. She cast him a questioning look, and he nodded. "But we have some very special news. We're going to..." She waited for him to finish the sentence.

"Get married," Luke concluded for her.

"I hope that's okay," Jane asked Zoey.

"Yay!"

"We'll be moving into Jane's house," Luke added.

His daughter gave an excited hop. "With Stopgap?"

"You bet," Jane said. "And would you mind if I asked you to be my flower girl?"

"Oh, thank you! Yes, yes, please!" She raced into Jane's arms, and they hugged until tears ran down their faces and Luke embraced them both.

They dressed the baby, grabbed the champagne and walked to the Lorenzes' house. Zoey trotted gleefully between her father and future stepmother.

Puffy pink and blue bells festooned the front of Number 18. Neighbors spilled onto the porch and, when someone spotted them, cheers went up. Obviously, Brooke had spread the word.

"It's the happy couple!"

"Congratulations!"

"Can I take photographs at the wedding?" Carly called, and they nodded, laughing.

Others swarmed around with warm wishes, including Bart. As the two men shook hands, Luke was glad they could stay on good terms.

Tess, the attorney, offered to help with Tina's adoption as her wedding present, while Cynthia Lieberman congratulated them, too. After the initial burst of greetings died down, Sherry took Jane and Luke aside.

"Wendy Clark approached me about the Annie Raft Memorial Clinic," she told them over a glass of champagne. "I'm going to talk to some of my old friends who're darn good fund-raisers. We should adopt this as a project."

"That's tremendous," Luke said.

"She told me about the MRI and the nanobots project, too," Sherry enthused. "That could really save lives."

"What project?" Jane glanced between them. Maybe she should have asked more questions when he mentioned the MRI.

Luke filled her in. "I discussed it with Wendy yesterday and she jumped right on it. Nothing's certain yet, of course, but she's very eager to have us participate."

Carly and Brittany intervened, urging them to admire the new Web pages. Since he'd already seen them, Luke stood back and let the others get a good view.

The cheery hum of voices filled a house perfumed with chocolate and raspberry. In the living room, he spotted Zoey telling Suzy of her plans to be a flower girl. In a portable playpen, Tina chewed on her new bunny and leaned against Marlene.

A sense of euphoria enveloped Luke, as if the champagne was a little stronger than usual. The feeling grew as he navigated through the crowd toward his wife-to-be.

This, he realized, was what happiness felt like.

Slipping his arm around Jane's waist, he couldn't believe that he'd been too obtuse to notice what was right under his nose. For a doctor, he'd come perilously close to missing the most important diagnosis of his life.

Which was, of course, an incurable case of love.

Romantic
SUSPENSE

Sparked by Danger, Fueled by Passion.

The Agent's Secret Baby

by *USA TODAY* bestselling author
Marie Ferrarella

TOP SECRET DELIVERIES

Dr. Eve Walters suddenly finds herself pregnant
after a regrettable one-night stand and turns to an
online chat room for support. She eventually learns
the true identity of her one-night stand: a DEA agent
with a deadly secret. Adam Serrano does not want
this baby or a relationship, but can fear for Eve's
and the baby's lives convince him that this is what
he has been searching for after all?

Available October wherever books are sold.

**Look for upcoming titles in
the TOP SECRET DELIVERIES miniseries**
The Cowboy's Secret Twins by Carla Cassidy—November
The Soldier's Secret Daughter by Cindy Dees—December

Visit Silhouette Books at www.eHarlequin.com

SRS27650

REQUEST YOUR FREE BOOKS!

2 FREE NOVELS PLUS 2 FREE GIFTS!

HARLEQUIN®

American ★ Romance®

Love, Home & Happiness!

HAR09R2

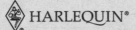

HARLEQUIN®

American ★ Romance®

COMING NEXT MONTH
Available October 13, 2009

#1277 TOP GUN DAD by Ann DeFee
Men Made in America
Flying missions for the U.S. Air Force seems easy compared to being a
single father. Between dealing with teenage angst and starting a new life in
Oklahoma, pilot Chad Cassavetes has no time for romance. But then he meets
Kelbie Montgomery, an intriguing single mom who has sworn off military men.
Can Chad change Kelbie's rules of engagement—and become her very own
top gun?

#1278 A BABY FOR MOMMY by Cathy Gillen Thacker
The Lone Star Dads Club
Mealtimes were mayhem before busy single father Dan Kingsland took on a
personal chef. Too bad that when he hired the wonderful Emily Stayton he didn't
notice the baby bump under her coat. Now the single mother-to-be is leaving
Fort Worth after Thanksgiving…unless Dan can convince Emily that her baby
needs a dad, as much as his kids need a mother.

#1279 MISTLETOE HERO by Tanya Michaels
4 Seasons in Mistletoe
Arianne Waide has always felt an important part of her small-town Georgia
community. She wants Gabe Sloan to feel that way, too—which is why she's
making the resident bad boy her personal mission. But old rumors still follow
Gabe, keeping him an outsider in his own town. Until, that is, he has a chance
to show everyone what it takes to be a *real* hero.

#1280 THE LITTLEST MATCHMAKER by Dorien Kelly
The last thing busy bakery owner and single mother Lisa Kincaid needs is
to start dating again. So why is the Iowa widow starting to look at sexy
construction-company owner Kevin Decker in a new light? Their friendship is
about to blossom into something new and exciting—with a little push from a
four-year-old Cupid!

www.eHarlequin.com

HARCNMBPA0909